INTERESTING PEOPLE

A SMALL TOWN ON THE CONNECTICUT RIVER IN VERMONT, BRATTLEBORO IS A CULTURAL HAVEN. WITH THE MUSIC OF KING TUFF AND THE LENTILS IN MIND, ARTIST LUKE THOMAS PRODUCED THIS WARPED VISION OF HIS HOMETOWN.

CONVERSE

THE PITCHFORK REVIEW

=━┤ *TPR!* ├━=

Contents

Control P

Contributors

In this issue, there are visual contributions from Tim Barber, Boogie, Jörg Brüggemann, Molly Butterfoss, Jem Cohen, Daniel Cronin, Autumn De Wilde, Cali Thornhill DeWitt, Alan Del Rio Ortiz, Cheryl Dunn, Paley Fairman, Jules Faure , Debra Friedman, Julian Gilbert, Steve Gullick, Paul Hornschemeier, Michael Jang, Jean Jullien, Hannah K. Lee, Jessica Lehrman, Ryan Mastro, Ryan McGinley, Chad Moore, Steele O'Neal, Steve Perille, Ron Regé Jr., Michael Renaud, Jess Rotter, David C. Sampson, Johnny Sampson, Jamel Shabazz, Noah Sheldon, Christian Storm, Sam Taylor, Melchior Tersen, Wolfgang Tillmans, and Jessica Viscius.

Demi Adejuyigbe, Joshua Alston, Liz Armstrong, Andy Beta, Chris Chafin, Ian Cohen, Laia Garcia, Sasha Geffen, Vivien Goldman, Jayson Greene, Ian Harris, Keith Harris, Jessica Hopper, Christina Lee, Zack Lipez, Steve Lowenthal, Michael Miller, J.R. Nelson, Erin Osmon, Ed Park, Mike Powell, Marianna Ritchey, Dylan Tupper Rupert, Scott Seward, Julianne Escobedo Shepherd, Brandon Stosuy, Estelle Tang, David Turner, Jeff Weiss, and Lindsay Zoladz wrote things for this issue.

About this issue's cover

Hanging in *Pitchfork*'s conference room is a six-foot-long fluorescent vignette of the bizarre and grotesque tradition we all know as the summer music festival. *Festival Frenzy* (Nobrow Press) was created by Kyle Platts to give us something to zone out to while our eyes glaze over in budget meetings, and we thought a continuation of his idea would be the perfect way to illustrate our first summer issue. This tradition has been depicted in countless ways over the years (our favorite being Jason Frederick's fantastic *Chicago Reader* covers during our annual festival). This is our entry into that time-honored canon, courtesy of **Kyle Platts**.

EIGHT SIMPLE TRICKS FOR FIGHTING CASSETTE NOSTALGIA. NUMBER 3 WILL BLOW YOUR BALLS OFF.

WHAT KIND OF SELF-LOATHING THINK PIECE ARE YOU?

THIS TURTLE SWAM INSIDE ST. VINCENT'S TOUR SUBMARINE, AND YOU WON'T BELIEVE WHAT HAPPENED NEXT.

WHY THIS 56-YEAR-OLD MAN ISN'T BUYING ULTRAVIOLENCE ON 180-GRAM VINYL

ISSUE 3 ILLUSTRATION BY JEAN JULLIEN

Ryan Dombal

Contributing Editor

Evan Kindley

Contributing Editor

Molly Butterfoss

Art Direction

Joy Burke

Jessica Viscius

Graphic Design

Erik Sanchez

Photo Editor

Mark Beasley

Andrew Gaerig

Neil Wargo

Developers

Ryan Schreiber

FOUNDER AND CEO

Christopher Kaskie

PRESIDENT AND PUBLISHER

Michael Renaud

CREATIVE DIRECTOR

Mark Richardson

EDITOR IN CHIEF OF PITCHFORK.COM

Brandon Stosuy

MANAGING EDITOR

J.C. Gabel

EDITOR AND ASSOCIATE PUBLISHER

Jessica Hopper

SENIOR EDITOR

Ryan Kennedy

OPERATIONS AND COPY EDITOR

RJ Bentler

VP, Video Programming

Matthew Frampton

VP, Business

Matthew Dennewitz

VP, Technology

Megan Davey

VP, Finance

Brian Fitzpatrick

Logistics

Ash Slater

Brandon Stosuy

Events & Support

Evan Kindley

Sybil Perez

Proofreaders

Colophon

Set in typefaces from Klim Type Foundry (*klim.co.nz*), Lineto (*lineto.com*), Colophon Foundry (*colophon-foundry.org*), and Grilli Type (*grillitype.com*). Printed on Finch Fine bright white antique 70# text, porcelainECO 30 gloss100# text, and Mohawk Superfine white eggshell 70# text. Cover is printed on Sappi McCoy silk 100# cover.

The Pitchfork Review No. 3, July 2014. Published four times a year by Pitchfork Media Inc. 3317 W. Fullerton Ave., Chicago, IL 60647. All material ©2014. All rights reserved. Subscription rate in the US for 4 issues is $49.99. Foreign subscriptions are $128.99. *The Pitchfork Review* is distributed by Publishers Group West. Printed by Palmer Printing Inc. 739 S. Clark St., Chicago, IL 60605. All advertising inquiries should be sent to Matthew Frampton at mattf@pitchfork.com. *The Pitchfork Review* does not read or accept unsolicited submissions, nor does it assume responsibility for the views expressed by its contributors. Contact info@thepitchforkreview.com for general information and reprints. Reproduction in whole or in part without permission is prohibited. *The Pitchfork Review* is a registered trademark of Pitchfork Media Inc.

ISBN-13: 978-09913992-2-2

Whatʼs it mean to be a music fan? A lot of listening and reading, sure. Shelves of records or hard drives stuffed with MP3s or a certain amount of bandwidth dedicated to streaming, likely. A full calendar of live shows. T-shirts, patches. But fandom is also about community, about finding yourself surrounded by people with a similar passion and using that shared experience as a springboard for connection. This communal feeling is something thatʼs important to us internally at *Pitchfork*, particularly how it fits into the broader community we share with our readers.

We hope *The Pitchfork Review* serves to extend and enrich our involvement in that shared community, giving us new passions, ideas, or conversations to expand upon. This issue of *The Review* has a few pieces that touch on these ideas, of what happens between people when thereʼs a shared interest in a sound or band or scene, and how we map our personal interests and desires onto the wider world. We hope you enjoy it, slot it on your shelf, and come back to that feeling for years to come. Weʼll see you next time.

Letters

Dear Pitchfork *Editors,*

I am deeply emotionally invested in disliking either Win Butler or Wayne Coyne. But it has recently been brought to my attention that a) In much the same way that "my" sports team winning is no actual reflection of my worth, musicians aren't my friends, and the value I assign them should perhaps be based solely upon aesthetics. And b) Both men are kind of jerks.

Please Advise,
FAN IN DISTRESS

—

To Pitchfork *Editors,*

Hail. In your recent review of our cassette, *Non Infernales,* you refer to our lyrics as "problematic." While my partner, Beholder Eye Stalk, and myself care not for the simpering death whine of Jewish (I use the term purely as descriptive; I assume "Kelly," in this case, is Jewish) media, I feel the need to correct your entirely erroneous assumptions about us and the diabolical anti-beliefs we stand for. Our previous splits with Satanic Mongrel Stomper and Heroic Quisling, as well as our recorded output on Burzum Shirt Records, are entirely beside the point. The song "Cosmic Vomitorium of Judennacht" is using the Jews *hypothetically* making the anti-universal force of true light vomit in a *metaphorical* way. Only a simpleminded fool from a shallow gene pool, incapable of rational thought, would think otherwise. Our band, Holocaustium, is most certainly *not* a National Socialist Black Metal band. We are, in fact, apolitical. It is laughable (laugh OUT LOUD) to even consider us as fascists, as we are each 1/5th Cherokee on our mother's side and have, in fact, seen multiple episodes of *Will and Grace.* We closed our eyes during the "Grace" part. Again, LAUGH OUT LOUD! I kid. I am well aware of your people's (music critics') love of humor. Your weakness sickens but still Holocaustium accommodates. Please retract your Jew (again, purely descriptive) lies. We have 40 more tapes to sell.

Hail,
BLACK PERSON DISLIKER
(it's a family name)

—

Dear Hipster Douchebags,

I dare you guys to print this letter. But I know you won't because you only liked letters to the editor when they were cool, right? Right? You just stand there, smoking American Spirits in the record store in your mom's basement, judging the rest of us for liking actually good music. Have you ever even HEARD music or are your ears elitist dicks like the rest of you?

Hipsters like you are the reason that music sucks and Angela broke up with me. She was the only kind thing in my life.

Sincerely,
NOT A HIPSTER EVER

—

Dear Editors at Pitchfork,

I am writing to draw attention to a problem with the metrics of your recent 7.3 review of the new Spiral Stairs double album, *Off Time is in Time.* According to my calculations (+4 for being Pavement related; -5.8 for not being Steve Malkmus; +.9 for being on Siltbreeze; -.9 for being on Siltbreeze; +3 for ambition of double album; +2 for being tangentially affiliated with the '90s; -3 from all album scores for it not actually, at this present time, being the '90s; +6 for Steve Keene album art; no effect on score for being mixed but not recorded at Electrical Audio) the album should have received an 8.3 and Best New Music. I realize that *Pitchfork* has had to change (i.e., compromise) with the times and the general degradation of culture, but I would appreciate it if you would amend the score.

And please go back to mentioning This Heat in every review. I miss that.

Thank You For Your Time,
T. PRESS

—

BY ZACK LIPEZ

Dear Editors at Pitchfork,

Hello. I am writing because, as the guitarist of Revolution Summer, the tri-state area's most, forgive me, embraced DC-themed wedding band, I am the sole proprietary owner of the term "emo revival." Revolution Summer, which I formed in 1994, while recovering from that Unrest/Pussy Galore unpleasantness, is my sole livelihood besides my full-time job as the number one provider of "This is Not a Fugazi Shirt" shirts for the, currently defunct but (true to the spirit of '85) hope springs eternal, Sessions catalog.

I also get a little money from my family.

Please be advised that "emo revival," besides being the name of our first, second, and third EP of wedding-appropriate emotional hardcore covers, is a copyrighted brand, and I therefore request in the strongest terms that you please stop using it. Please *also* be advised that I have many friends who briefly went to law school.

I have sent an identical letter to *Alternative Press.*

Cold Rice Forever,
JEFF
(not that Jeff)
(or that one)

—

Dear Pitchfork,

In the current profile of Fever Ray, by one Lindsay Zoladz, 2,000-plus words are expended on the artist without ONCE telling me what the artist actually sounds like. There are comparisons to Brian Eno, Fad Gadget, and Weeknd, but (and I shouldn't have to tell you this) those are all boys. HOW CAN A GIRL SOUND LIKE A BOY. Not once in this entire "article" did Miss Zoladz tell me what *female* musicians Fever Ray sound like. If you don't compare a female musician to other female musicians then how am I, the consumer, to know where I stand? This confusion you caused has filtered into the rest of my life, and now, because I don't have adequate points of comparison for Fever Ray and other musicians who share some vague musical touchstones and have the same genitalia, I am putting food in my butt and wearing shoes on my head. Thanks for nothing.

Sincerely,
A FELLOW CRITIC

—

rip COOL

Q&A with Joel Dinerstein on the death of cool

BY JESSICA HOPPER

For the last 18 years, Joel Dinerstein has been teaching "The History of Cool" at Tulane University, where he is the James H. Clark Endowed Chair in American Civilization. He's the co-curator of *American Cool*, a collection of 100 photos of icons of cool—including Jay-Z, Chrissie Hynde, and Bob Dylan—on exhibit at the National Portrait Gallery until September 7. He spoke to *The Pitchfork Review* about the exhibit and the death of cool from his office in New Orleans.

IN YOUR EXPERTISE, WHO IS THE COOLEST LIVING AMERICAN MUSICIAN?

I get asked this a lot. The only way I ever answer this question is to say that if you ask people who's the greatest symbol of American cool, the two answers you get are Miles Davis and James Dean—Dean way more than Miles, for obvious reasons.

HOW DID YOU GET TO THIS LIST OF 100?

We asked film scholars, pop culture scholars, friends. We can argue about who's not on the list, but everyone who is passes the test—the rubric of the exhibit about artistic vision, rebellion, iconic power. Shortly before we had to turn in the final list, I had dinner with a bunch of journalists and writers, and they threw all these names at me. Every person they named was on there, except one: Bill Murray. I was embarrassed we'd forgotten him somehow. I can't tell you who we bumped to include him—it was a months-long process. There was a big fight about Jerry Garcia—he is one of the most divisive characters in any discussion.

HAS COOL BECOME MORE ELUSIVE NOW?

Ultimately, for me, cool existed from 1940 to 1980. That was a time when underground meant something, and it wasn't ironic or cheesy. "Revolutionary" meant something, even though it might be laughable now. And cool ends in the '80s, for identifiable reasons. Cool was about someone who sees the world uniquely and differently and then takes us along for the ride. I am not sure anyone is invested in that anymore. One of the things that gets missed in discussions is people think the meaning of cool is trans-historical, that it doesn't change with generations. What was cool in the '50s—Brando cool—is different from the '80s Prince cool. The youth generation needs something else in that moment that is determined by historical contingencies. So, maybe what we did with this exhibit is historicize cool at the moment it's ending.

IF THAT'S THE CASE, THEN WHAT IS COOL'S EULOGY?

I try not to be this cynical, but it's social media and Facebook. It's narcissism. People are so busy with their public identities they have no time to invest it in others or in who they're looking up to. Someone who gives you an image to emulate—someone you want to be like—and you use that model to experiment and change who you are. Between the ages of 17–25 you negotiate your identity through these role models. Even the brightest, smartest, most artistic students now seem to be really self-absorbed at the level of curating identity and public utterances, which seems to take away from how you emulate cultural figures, people who are transgressive and breach the social fabric for you.

BOOKS OF THE STARS ～LAIA GARCIA

WHAT HAVE YOU BEEN READING, HALEY BONAR?

I'm reading *The Goldfinch* by Donna Tartt. Her previous book *The Secret History* is one of my favorites. She's a master at creating an emotional experience that somehow becomes the reader's own. Sometimes I have to remind myself that it's just a book, and that these feelings can (supposedly) be left behind when I close it.

Wordy Motherfuckers

Who has the biggest vocabulary of them all?

BY ESTELLE TANG

PARQUET COURTS' NEW ALBUM, *SUNBATHING ANIMAL*, IS OUT. WE KNOW THEY'RE WORDY MOTHERFUCKERS, BUT HOW DO THEY RANK AMONG OTHER SESQUIPEDALIAN (THAT'S "LONG-WORD-LOVING" TO YOU) INDIE LYRICISTS?

Wordy motherfuckers: Of Montreal
Sample lyrics: "They had to pretend to ignore the large grotesque arthropods"
Meaning: Arthropods are invertebrate animals of the large phylum Arthropoda, such as insects, spiders, or crustaceans.
 Dictionary rating: One dictionary. Someone was paying attention in bio class.

Wordy motherfuckers: Parquet Courts
Sample lyrics: "Tanned slow and low in the amines of guilt"; "Steps and gables, steeples"
Meaning: Amines are organic compounds derived from ammonia. A gable is the triangular upper part of a wall.
 Dictionary rating: Two dictionaries. Props for just casually slipping some tricky shit in.

Wordy motherfucker: Fiona Apple
Sample lyrics: "My derring-do allows me to do the rigadoon around you"
Meaning: "Derring-do" means action displaying heroic courage. The "rigadoon" is "a lively dance for couples ... of Provençal origin."
 Dictionary rating: Three dictionaries. I mean, they rhyme and everything.

Wordy motherfucker: Joanna Newsom
Sample lyrics: "As they wetly bow with hydrocephalitic listlessness"; "the mantle of her diluvian shoulders"
Meaning: "Hydrocephalitic" is a Newsom-coined variant of "hydrocephalic," which is the adjectival form of a condition in which fluid accumulates in the brain. "Diluvian" means relating to floods.
 Dictionary rating: Four dictionaries. Making up words is some Shakespeare-level game.

 Definitions taken from the Oxford Dictionaries.

YELLE SPEAKS

BY CHRIS CHAFIN

Have you ever gotten sucked into watching a really dumb French movie? One that grabs you with its abandon, its shamelessness, and the utter seriousness with which it treats having fun? So it is with Yelle, the dance-pop French trio, about to release their third record, this time on mega-producer Dr. Luke's Kemosabe Records. Their songs are at once light candy-colored nothings and deadly serious pieces of music with a high-art edge. We spoke with singer Julie Budet and producer Jean-François Perrier (a.k.a. GrandMarnier) on a recent spring afternoon. All conversations preserved in Budet's devastatingly charming, halting English, whenever possible.

WHAT WAS THE LAST YOUTUBE TUTORIAL THAT YOU WATCHED, AND WHY?

Julie Budet: I think the last tutorial was how to plug—how do you call that? A lamp! Because I like to do things like that in my house. Fixation? I didn't know the terms in English. Wire. All the things in your house—fix little things like lamps, electricity.

WHAT WAS THE LAST THING YOU LOOKED UP ON GOOGLE AND WHY?

JB: I looked at pictures of Sasquatch! Festival because we played there a few days ago. I'd heard a lot of stuff about the place and how beautiful it was. But I didn't really know what to expect. It was beautiful in pictures, but it was incredible in life.

SO, YOU WEREN'T LOOKING FOR PICTURES OF YOURSELF?

JB: No! I don't like to see pictures or videos. I'm always like [makes her face as disgusting as it can look]. It's not always nice. You are like, bleech!

WHAT'S MORE DISGUSTING, AMERICA OR FRANCE?

JB: France. I don't know if you heard the news, but it's kind of hard to be French right now. We had to vote last weekend for the European Parliament, and the [far-right] National Front won. When we heard the results, we were in the van and were all depressed, like, "What the fuck!" We are living in a racist country.

WHAT'S ONE FRENCH STEREOTYPE THAT'S ACTUALLY TRUE?

JB: The smoking, especially in Paris.
Jean-François Perrier: It's part of the style. Especially DJs. They don't have much to do, so they smoke, and you have smoke in your face all night.

WHAT'S THE LAST REALLY EXPENSIVE THING YOU BOUGHT?

JB: My car? It's not expensive.

MORE EXPENSIVE THAN A SHIRT, I'M SURE.

JB: Right, but it's not an expensive car. It's a Nissan Cube. It's dark purple. I discovered this car in Japan, and I thought it was really cute. I saw a lot of them in Los Angeles. But it's not popular at all in France. I think there are just two of us in Paris with the car. I love it.

JULIE, YOU'VE BEEN ON TOUR WITH KATY PERRY AND IN A FILM WITH A MAN IN A CHICKEN COSTUME. WHICH FELT MORE NATURAL?

JB: Maybe the chicken?
[Furious French back and forth between JP and JB]
JB: Sorry, I did not understand the question.
JP: Maybe it was touring for us was more normal.
JB: But it was kind of crazy for us?
JP: Still, more normal than being in a film with a man in a chicken costume.

WHAT HAVE YOU BEEN READING, NENEH CHERRY?

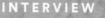

I have just read and loved *Ghana Must Go* by Taiye Selasi, and I'm currently reading *The Orchardist* by Amanda Coplin— both are novels. *The Orchardist* is set in the Northwestern U.S. in the twentieth century. A loner lives for his apples and apricots and finds two pregnant girls stealing … the tale is building beautifully so far. I'm still addicted to bookshops. I love the smell of them, the words all around spinning tales—information, knowledge, and adventure. They're my favorite places to escape to. There's a great literary show here in Sweden called *Babel*. I discover great new writers and books every Monday when it airs. When I am deep in a book, I will read during any spare minute: planes, trains, cars, cozying up in bed, at the beach.

ANNOYING SUMMER SONGS

Various, "Summertime" (George Gershwin)
… the livin' is easy, fish are—TURN OFF SONG NOW

ANNOYING SUMMER SONGS

Mungo Jerry, "In the Summertime"
Sorry, I'm too distracted—are those muttonchops or "dundrearies"?

ANNOYING SUMMER SONGS

Elvis Costello, "The Other Side of Summer"
Cogent yet catchy meditation on the American dream/nightmare (Not.)

10-Word Reviews by Brandon Stosuy, Ed Park, and Michael Miller

((((((((Here's Your Future, Today))))))))
By Keith Harris

We listen to pop radio today to learn how we will remember the present tomorrow. That's why a hated hit single summons an acid dread no sucky multiplex blockbuster ever can. Innocuous yet inescapable, songs define who we will someday be, as surely as snapshots of our worst teen haircuts. I mean, if you hear Robin Thicke squeal, "You the hottest bitch in this place" on the radio at the exact time you learn your grandma has died, then, seriously, good luck with your life after that.

And so, as "Fancy" and "Problem" tag team the charts, some fret that Iggy Azalea's sour drawl will be the lingering aftertaste of 2014. An Australian blonde with T.I.'s flow and Nicki Minaj's ass who dresses like Alicia Silverstone in *Clueless* while competently inflecting syllables Ctrl-V'ed from Rap Genius and 2009 YouTube comments, Iggy will surely someday exasperate cultural historians studying early twenty-first century American radio's convoluted efforts at bleaching its playlists.

"Fancy" truly belongs to Charli XCX, hopscotching atop synth-blips with brat-on-the-beat sass, her faux-teen wink deflating Iggy's grown-ass posturing. The bridge is where Charli lets on that, for all the champagne wishes and transcontinental itineraries that came before, she's really singing about post-prom hotel hijinks, like raiding a minibar and calling room service. The karaoke video for "Fancy" should display every word of Charli's chorus and then, when Iggy starts in, the screen should just read "[rapping]."

Iggy's even less of a threat to Ariana Grande's giddily feverish "Problem," a wobbly Jenga tower of a track that stays upright despite all the jazzmatazz horn hooks and En Vogue breakdowns stacked precariously on top. Ariana sings like she's standing on tippy-toes to reach those high notes. Her awkwardness is a reminder that imitation Mariah is more fun than the real thing in 2014, a fact that even Mariah seems to accept on her new album (even if that knowledge hasn't helped her score a hit). Nah, I don't know why Big Sean's here either, but let's pretend Ariana was just helping him get over his breakup with Naya.

> **SEAN:** [Bounds into studio] Hey Ari, I got those rhymes you wanted me to spit.
> **ARIANA:** [Giggles. Extending his name to three or four syllables] Se-ea-an! You are so funny! Here, I just need you to whisper this line creepily.
> **SEAN:** [Pouts] Oh. Okay. [A deep breath] So, hey, you wanna maybe get coffee sometime or something?
> **ARIANA:** [Hugs him as though he is an oversized stuffed animal] Oh Sean! You are so sweet! You are [speaking as you would to a beloved pet] Such! A! Good! Friend!

No less jaunty a taunt than "Problem," Paramore's "Ain't It Fun" inverts the riff from Bananarama's "Cruel Summer" to spunky rather than spooky effect. Lyrically, it's "Like a Rolling Stone" rewritten as one of those cranky truth-bomb commencement addresses decrying entitled millennials that your uncle posts to Facebook with his misspelled, all-caps endorsement. But Hayley Williams is pop's most buoyant buzzkill, yoinking the privilege out from under some snot whose gender goes unspecified. Gotta be a boy though, right?

Then again, if it's boys you want ... well, the radio's got plenty of boys you don't want. At 23, Ed Sheeran is not a Bieber, not yet a Timberlake—though with Pharrell aggressively amassing chop-funk acoustic guitars, "Sing" is clearly intended as Sheeran's "Like I Love You." Instead, a falsetto chorus suggestive of both the Stones' "Miss You" and Rod Stewart's "Do Ya Think I'm Sexy?" results in an accidental tribute to rich white men demanding that you watch them dance.

As for Jason Derulo, he first attracted public attention by repeatedly howling his own name, like a shell of a man sitting alone in a dark room trying to remember who he once was. He's ID'ing himself less frequently these days—a questionable move, since singing "Jason Derulo" is probably the only thing Chris Brown can't do better. Dude's got less game than a Tinder bot: "Talk Dirty" is about how he gets more action in foreign countries because the women there don't understand what he's saying, and "Wiggle" is the worst thing to happen to butts since wedgies, since hemorrhoids, since Iggy Azalea. And it's got a verse from Snoop, in case you doubt that "leering creep" is a viable long-term career.

"John Legend" is also a viable long-term career. The most tendentious instruction manual for how to stay married to a supermodel since Billy Joel's "A Matter of Trust," Legend's "All of Me" is apparently custom-tooled to soundtrack the first dance at starter marriages all across America this summer. Whenever I hear it, I think of something Lil Jon once said, and I ask myself, "Turn down for this? For *this*?"

That same question resurfaces when I hear Nico & Vinz's "Am I Wrong," which envisions an alternate reality in which Sting wasn't a pompous pseudo and subsequently The Police were actually The Outfield. And again when I hear Sam Smith, a Stray Cats hairdo dude who ponders each syllable of "Stay with Me" with such mannered precision you can practically see him squinting to read the Italian notations on his sheet music. (He also cut a duet version with Mary J. Blige, which is about as foolhardy as Macklemore asking Rakim to get on the mic.)

But really, what should you turn down for? After six months of "Turn Down for What," Lil Jon's blurted query remains as unanswerable as any koan. After a brief inventory of weed and liquor, that four-word challenge doesn't tell us it can't stop or that it won't stop—it just doesn't stop. DJ Snawke's cross-fader wanking is as corny as Steve Miller's guitar imitating a wolf whistle on "The Joker"; as corny as the Baha Men woofing over the loudspeakers during a pitching change; as corny as the movements your body will make if you're foolish enough to try to dance to it. But "Turn Down for What" is how I'll remember 2014 five years from now, and I guarantee you I still won't have an answer. ✐

••••• DESIRED FREQUENCIES   102 JAMZ THE HIP-HOP STATION   BY DAVID TURNER •••••

Driving through North Carolina on I-85, the only means for excitement are BBQ billboards and signs warning of looming construction. But tuning the FM dial to 102 JAMZ puts listeners at the center of the rap world while passing between Burlington and Salisbury.

Transmitted from Greensboro—where other neighboring broadcasts slip into conflicting signals—WJMH 102 JAMZ, a mid-major mainstream rap station, turns it up with uninterrupted mixes of Future and DJ Mustard deep cuts. The station's catholic tastes always select the right throwback track for standstill traffic. Should Shawty Lo's 2008 hit "Dunn Dunn" remain on rap playlists in 2014? 102 JAMZ emphatically argues, "Yes."

Instead of reflecting the popularity of *Billboard* charts, the station follows its own barometer: the station was quick to trends from the Bay Area (Sage the Gemini's "Gas Pedal") to Atlanta (Young Thug's "Stoner") to Chicago (Katie Got Bandz's "Pop Out"). With a pulse on rap trends, the station also knows its listeners. Did the program directors sense you had a bad night and played Ty$'s "Paranoid" to salve your wounded ego or heart? Nah, but in the moment, it doesn't matter. Behind the wheel, listing to 102 JAMZ, it'll be loud enough so all passersby know what's up. ✐

VINYL GEMS IN
THE CUTOUT BIN
BY SCOTT SEWARD

Michael Quatro

Dancers, Romancers, Dreamers & Schemers

(Prodigal Records, 1976)

AS I write this, the latest eBay auction of Michael Quatro's *Dancers, Romancers, Dreamers & Schemers* has ended on the princely sum of $2.31. Kind of a sad number. Sadder still, the person who bought it might have overpaid. There are records that are underrated, and there are records that aren't rated at all. This is the latter. Which is a shame! Michael himself is a hustler, booster, lover, and one-man band. Blessed with righteous musical sisters, the Quatro family rocked Detroit for years before Michael helped little sister Suzi get a record deal and find her way to international glam-rock stardom. Mike never hit it that big (nor did big sis Patti, who joined a revamped glam version of all-female band Fanny in 1974), but his first records were dug in elite stoner dens around Detroit and the rest of the country at the dawn of the '70s. There is a very real possibility that you could find Mike's first three, over-the-top orchestral astral-prog records for a buck if you look for a bit. But they are all worth hearing. Mike brought Detroit to prog in the same way Suzi brought it to glam. They had that Motor City rhythm, and no matter how ornate Mike's keyboard work got

(and, oh, man, did it get ornate), there was always a rock-bottom funk and swing to his music that all the Brits in capes at the time could never even dream of approximating.

Dancers is the last of Mike's '70s records to really go for the street-prog gold. Recorded for Motown's Prodigal Records subsidiary, the album begins with astral falsetto soul and Mike beckoning the children of tomorrow to touch him today and it's only a *little* creepy. He could have sold this song to The Dells or any number of bespoke-suited soul smoothies and made some quick cash. The second track "Stripper" is about ... a stripper. It's slow and low lysergic funk, and god only knows how many keyboards are on this recording. There is Moog, theremin, phazer, Mellotron, organ, piano, and MiniKorg, etc., layered throughout this album. The first real showstopper is "Rollerbach," where the funky phantom of the Detroit skating rink meets badass drum breaks, booty synth drops, and acidic guitar leads that intertwine with chicken-pecked Deep South henhouse axes. And there is Bach. The second side gets a little Chopin. *Somehow* Mike makes the light classical touches work.

Don't ask me how. The album is full of them, and they are never a drag. They're fun! And he's a sweet ivory tickler.

The most epic of all epic set pieces is the track "Ancient Ones." It's a masterpiece of the form. The form being heavy, seven-minute psychedelic prog songs that have riffs for days. Riffs like woozy anthems to evil gods complete with spoken recitation and maniacal laughter (provided by Pavlov's Dog singer, David Surkamp, one of the few rock singers who can make Geddy Lee sound like Barry White). The song slows down in some crazy proto-screw music fashion, and then sloooowly starts back up again. You wonder if you heard what you heard. You did. Mike was cool like that. The only misstep is the drippy ballad "One by One," which drags down the record. But you need one flaw in a work of art, or you will offend God. Everyone knows that. Mike's later albums are safer. He was still reaching for the brass ring and looking for a hit. It never really happened, but his albums from that time—even the later disco-pop and funk-rock efforts—are well worth that hard-earned dollar of yours. ✐

WHAT HAVE YOU BEEN READING, MYKKI BLANCO?

I am currently reading *Passionate Journey: The Spiritual Autobiography of Satomi Myodo*. It's about a woman's search for enlightenment in modern Japan. She was born in 1896, died in 1978, but in her lifetime she rejected the cultural tradition of being a "good wife" and "wise mother," and chose to become a disciple of a Shinto priest, a shamaness, and an oracle during exorcisms. My grandparents on my father's side are very spiritual people and are fascinated with folk tales, epic sagas, and any kind of sociological religious study. They have stacks of books of this ilk. I seem to have inherited the taste for the subject matter. I'm interested in the fantastical nature of reality.

SWANS NORSE VOYAGE

VESSEL Viking ship
DESTINATION The fjords of Norway
ITINERARY At the end of day one, Michael Gira leads tantric yoga atop Mt. Skårasalen's summit while Swans improvise a six-hour battle hymn. Days two through four depend on whether you've pleased the gods enough for them to free you from the fog.
COST One (1) mammal skull or fresh human umbilical cord

THE KNIFE PRESENTS: THE *SHAKING THE HABITUAL* VOLCANO PLUNGE

VESSEL Your body, the ways society has programmed you to feel about your body
DESTINATION Into the fire
ITINERARY Burn wealth, burn gender roles, burn consumerism, burn competition, burn hate, burn hierarchy.
COST Everything you have ever held onto to construct your identity under capitalism

SASHA GEFFEN

ICEAGE TUNDRA CRAWL

VESSEL Enormous snowmobile
DESTINATION Alaskan wilds
ITINERARY In a three-day tour of the cruel northern state, the boys from Copenhagen lead flensing workshops, a wolf-wrestling tourney, and the First Annual Frost Mosh. The hot toddies are free but the blood you lose is your problem.
COST A few extremities, probably

Dream World Music Expeditions

a.k.a. alternatives to the Weezer Cruise

ST. VINCENT DEEP-SEA TRENCH DIVE

VESSEL Military submarine
DESTINATION Five miles below sea level
ITINERARY Surfing deepwater jet streams, serenading anglerfish with a live cut of "Cruel," internet detox. Matte lipstick and futuristic fascist military uniform required for entry.
COST All of your mind, all of your loves

WHAT HAVE YOU BEEN READING, CLAIRE EVANS (YACHT)?

I am reading Tracy Kidder's *The Soul of a New Machine*, which profiles a group of engineers in Massachusetts in the early '80s as they build and bring to market a new 32-bit microcomputer. It's beautifully written, and set in a time before computers were so ubiquitous as to be invisible. It really brings to light how exponentially strange our current technological moment is. I've been a science journalist and science fiction critic for nearly a decade, so the books I read tend to be work-related, but I often pick something up because I feel, intuitively, that it will be good brain fuel for as-yet-unarticulated connections in future essays.

FUCK YOUR CAR

ATL'S BEST GAS STATIONS FOR MIXTAPES

by Christina Lee

Across Atlanta, where car and hip-hop culture intersect, 24-hour gas stations hawk mixtapes near the cigarettes and condoms.

Chevron Station No. 210042
1401 Moreland Ave. S.E.

Some compilations feature a single artist's current hits, while others offer fantasy-league lineups. This station offers both types, consistently.

RECENT PURCHASE
Lil Boosie's *Freedom*, 17 guest verses from his last year in jail.

Citgo Mini Mart Express
2989 Campbellton Rd. S.W.

Its selection spans the mainstream and underground, past and present. (It's also next to the JJ's Rib Shack of Goodie Mob's "Soul Food" fame.)

RECENT PURCHASE
Colors, 22 songs by Juicy J, Meek Mill and Kevin Gates — and only one being a collaboration.

Valero Food Mart
1989 Hosea L. Williams Dr. S.E.

The seedier past of Future's native Kirkwood lives on in its selection, despite a new coffee and craft-beer bar next door.

RECENT PURCHASE
ATL All Starz 15, its cover features Young Jeezy, Future and Young Thug staring ahead as three silver mics splash in promethazine.

BFF **MUSICAL FRIENDSHIPS EXPLAINED** BY JULIANNE ESCOBEDO SHEPHERD

PHOTOGRAPH BY JESSICA LEHRMAN

WHAT HAVE YOU BEEN READING, DAMIAN ABRAHAM (FUCKED UP)?

I just finished Mark Mazzetti's book *The Way of the Knife*. It's about the CIA post 9/11, and I really enjoyed it—as much as one can enjoy a book about other people's misery. I also just picked up Geoff Pevere's *Gods of the Hammer* about the band Teenage Head. I am so happy this book exists. They are one of the most important bands in Canadian history, and they're criminally overlooked. Let the canonization begin! Our van is eerily quiet most of the time, which is very conducive to reading or painful self-reflection—so it's my favorite place to read.

Singer Kelela and DJ/producer Total Freedom (née Ashland Mines) are Angelenos finding new avenues at the intersection of R&B and dance music. They are also best friends and muses. Both explain their BFF relationship to Julianne Escobedo Shepherd.

Kelela: A few years ago, Ashland invited me to this New Year's Eve party. He sent me a text: "4532 Palm Tree." Just an address. I walked into the greatest party I've ever been to in my life! The music that Ashland was playing made me be like, "Oh my god, yes." It was basically, like, grime edits and Mariah and Kelly Rowland with a cappella over them. It was what I wanted my original tracks to sound like. Then on my birthday, he sent me an email outlining how he thought of me musically, and what niche he sees I want to fill. It was so dead-on, I could have cried. It was so precisely what I wanted, and needed to hear, that somebody on the outside could hear what I was attracted to and be able to name it. I was like, "He sees meeeee!"

Total Freedom: That was a mass text, for sure, but obviously I wanted to hang. I met Kelela via her voice first—I heard the first demo she made for Teengirl Fantasy ["EFX"] and just lost it because I was really familiar with their music and it was something I never ever expected to hear a vocalist working with. It was such a weird track, and what Kelela did with it was really shocking to me. I got really worked up, like, "I can't believe this happened; it's so cool." The main thing that has always turned me on about Kelela's writing is just her being fearless, and being more excited about songs that are challenging. She always takes the hardest possible avenue and turns it around to make it really accessible and beautiful for anyone to listen to. From day one, that's what I've always been shocked and impressed by. And her presence has changed the way all these producers around me are working. Knowing what Kelela is capable of has really expanded the way people approach songwriting. I don't know anyone who would deny that.

Kelela: His SoundCloud is my homepage. I just need this reminder, like, "What are we on TODAY?" I get pumped, or if I watch an entire set, I'm ready to go and write a song. He makes me hear the palette of what I want to do more.

ADULT KICKBALL LEAGUES

Do your parents know you spend your weekends like this?

SUMMER

"I'm sorry," he said. "I don't find summer especially *inspiring*."

SLOW TO REALIZE

Wait, we're all dads now? I'm somehow just realizing this.

SOCKS WITH SHORTS

Why not wear long pants then? Ashamed of your ankles?

Skin Off My Back

Musical Self-Mortification in the Black Death

Like any thoughtful denizen of the Anthropocene, I am unhealthily interested in what historians call the "demographic crises" of yore. Perhaps none of these crises is more intriguing than the period of unusually intense mortality in the late Middle Ages, during which at least a third of Europe's population died of something that is now curable with antibiotics. The Black Death (contemporaries called it "The Great Death," which is also a good name for it but less metal) was a virulent episode of bubonic plague that began in 1347 or so, in the Middle East, and exploded like wildfire to cover the continent by 1351. It was spread by fleas, and if there's one thing we know for sure about medieval people, it's that they were constantly covered with fleas.

Imagine if a hundred million Americans died between now and the next presidential election. Whole towns and cities were completely emptied. Livestock wandered confused in abandoned fields. The plague toppled feudalism, and led to the birth of all kinds of new world orders, including the consolidation of church power, the monetization of labor and the economy, without which capitalism could not have been established, and the emergence of a specifically misogynist patriarchy in which reproductive crimes were often punishable by death.

One way this social disruption manifested was in the musical processions of flagellants that became common by 1349. Flagellants were religious penitents who sang mournful songs while whipping themselves bloody. These processions were not the first (nor the last) examples of penitential self-mortification in European culture (indeed, self-mortification is still practiced today by lots of Catholics the world over), but they were the first to go public. Flagellants turned their musical torture sessions into performances, mutilating themselves for all to see. Medieval Europeans loved a good public mutilation but usually these were done at the expense of criminals and witches; the spectacle of regular people rending their own flesh into ribbons while singing about Christ's torments made quite a different impression. And you thought going on tour was hard!

But what songs did they sing, these dread pilgrims of yore? Wouldn't you love to know? Well, it turns out that a priest named Hugo Spechtshart wrote some of them down in 1349. He notated them monophonically, which means there's only one melodic line and nothing else—although this doesn't preclude the possibility that they were accompanied by instruments, or that other sung harmonies were used at the performers' discretion. Tragically, these songs have not been commercially recorded, but you can look at the original manuscript online. My former UCLA professor Tamara Levitz translated one of the songs for me, and its lyrics do not disappoint. They beg God to "help us through [His] holy blood," and they proclaim, "We have to take the penitence upon ourselves" in order "to enter heaven." The songs appear to mainly be strophic, which means they have one melodic verse that repeats several times. This indicates they are probably derived from folk songs rather than church chants, which tend not to be so melodically repetitive or rhythmically regular.

While, again, these songs don't seem to have been recorded, there are a perhaps unsurprisingly large number of Swedish black metal bands with songs titled "Flagellant," which I urge you to listen to on YouTube. You could also watch Bergman's *The Seventh Seal*, in which there is a scene of flagellants terrifying some townspeople. They're singing the dies irae, which is a church chant, but for a chant it's unusually rhythmically regular and melodically repetitive—and its text describes the torments of hell—so it's a reasonably historically accurate choice, although it's unlikely so many non-priests would have all that Latin memorized.

Anyway, this is the kind of stuff we have to look forward to as society continues to crumble. ✐

Confusion
"Niggas in Paris"

Here Yeezy delivers the hanh de résistance (his Mona Yeeza, if you will) with a non sequitur on gorillas, as if reading it for the first time off a teleprompter.

Embarrassment & Pity
"Otis"

"You ain't accustomed to goin' through customs, you ain't been nowhere, hanh?" Imagine getting excited about seeing a rainbow then realizing you're talking to a blind person.

Punchline
"Monster"

Kanye's stand-up career is born in the same breath it dies, with a long "haaaaanh" sandwiched between memorable lines about pharaoh-fucking and sarcophagal pussy.

Belligerence
"Who Gon Stop Me"

"Kanye, you can't bring food into the theater." "Who gon' stop me, hanh?" "This is why we don't invite you places."

Deafness
"Power"

"We ain't got nothing to lose, motherfucker, we rollin'." What was that? "Hanh?" What did you say? "Motherfucker, we rollin'."

Fatherly
"Dark Fantasy"

Kanye throws out successive "hanhs" at the end of "Dark Fantasy," like a dad threatening to turn the car around on a road trip.

DESPERADOS & DISCO STRANGLERS

*THE EAGLES AND THE BIG DUMB
DREAM OF THE WEST*

BY IAN HARRIS

The Sweet Smell of Success

BY LIZ ARMSTRONG

Recent trend analysis shows a spike in celebrities and musicians hiring perfume houses to associate their names with "signature scents." Capitalizing on of-the-moment hype, many such fragrances tend to lack longevity. Here are our best bets on winning musician scents for the summer season and beyond.

WHITE LUNG
Skank Bait
Some flowers contain indoles, a dirty animalic molecule abundant in human feces. Skank Bait by White Lung combines dominant notes of the exotic and exhibitionist night-blooming excreta rose, a species that really ripens only after 3 a.m., with hints of Love's Baby Soft nostalgic powder, all topped with a metallic finish.

BECK
Moths at Dusk
One man's earthy, refined dash of Moths at Dusk powdered cologne is another man's handful of canyon sunset-scented dust slipping through his fingers. Also doubles as facial scrub dry shampoo.

Late last year, police were called to the home of Vernett Bader after she assaulted her sometimes-boyfriend and his buddy with a 14-inch serrated bread-knife. The fuse was lit, it turns out, when Bader asked the two men to "turn off the goddamn Eagles," which they had been listening to at considerable volume all day while beached on the sofa like engorged pythons guzzling beer after beer. They thereupon told Ms. Bader to "shut the hell up," at which point she retreated to the kitchen to rummage through the knife drawer.

Bader had, in a wonderful moment of Nietzschean clarity or, more likely, in a wonderful moment of slurred ranklement, acted out a scenario that has apparently been playing out in the American imagination since 1976's *Their Greatest Hits*. Which begs the question, what's so goddamn horrible about the Eagles that they could put a knife in someone's trembling hand? Moreover, why did the story catch fire on the AP wire and appear to provide so much cultural catharsis? I understand the vainglorious empty-headedness of the Eagles. The moral and romantic struggles that play out upon the chaparrals and arroyos of the Eagles' catalogue produce the kind of daydreams a pre-Pres. George W. Bush concocted while he watched oil jacks bob against the Houston skyline. I understand about how the Eagles seem inordinately interested in crafting the perfect boyfriend, insofar as the perfect boyfriend is a faux-desperado—impossible to tame—but one who suddenly coughs up a solitary red rose and a knee-buckling line he has written on his big, dumb, calloused hand: "I like the way your sparkling earrings lay against your skin so brown."

VH1's unofficial theory about the Eagles' rise to fame is that folk-rock essentially wore fans out with labor songs, civil rights anthems, and consciousness-expansion—and by 1972, everyone was ready to "take it easy," as it were, and maybe even let in a few warm rays of disco without altogether vacating the country-acoustic barn The Byrds, Neil Young, Poco, and The Flying Burrito Brothers had raised. And so it was the Eagles. Because the Eagles were California kids and they didn't give a shit. As Robert Christgau complained, they were "suave and synthetic—brilliant, but false."

Which is more or less true, in as far as John Ford's slow pan across Vera Miles and Monument Valley was false. Nobody has yet said the obvious thing about the Eagles—the most important thing—which is that they took up the rather complicated story of the West, just like Wallace Stegner and Joan Didion did, which is a story about a decent, uncomplicated cowboy who doesn't say much of anything except that he wants to build a house "at the bend in the river where the cottonwoods grow," only to discover later that the river dries up when it suits the corrupt irrigation board, and that the wide-open frontier was bought up and developed long before it became a thing to dream about.

Dried-up river beds, 10,000-acre nuclear test ranges, and the swelling depressions and preoccupations of suburbia—stoked by crippling freeways and the ripping Santa Ana winds—had become the cairns of Stegner's and Didion's magnificent unpackings of the post-frontier dreamworld by 1970. Meanwhile the folk singers of the era—those who the Eagles were apparently the antidote to—had overlooked the landscape, and the complex environmental issues facing the country—not to mention the complicating myths surrounding the Old West. "They paved paradise and put up a parking lot" gets at opportunism and environmental destruction all right, but it doesn't follow the money, and it absolves itself of its fair share of the blame. The Beach Boys' classic line, "Toothpaste and soap will make our oceans a bubble bath / So let's avoid an ecological aftermath" is just plain naïve. Nobody was scratching the surface of the West—the dream of it, the empty promise of it, and the gigantic starry scale of it—like the Eagles.

The Eagles knew, in other words, about the siphoning of Mono Lake and the gigawatts traveling across the desert from Lake Powell and a hundred other hydroelectric projects into Las Vegas and Los Angeles:

THEN THE CHILLY WINDS BLEW DOWN
ACROSS THE DESERT
THROUGH THE CANYONS OF THE COAST
TO THE MALIBU
WHERE THE PRETTY PEOPLE PLAY
HUNGRY FOR POWER
TO LIGHT THEIR NEON WAY
AND GIVE THEM THINGS TO DO

I don't mean to suggest the Eagles were in the business of hatching a sophisticated post-frontier literature. That said, in and among the platitudes, Spanish guitar fills, and solitary red roses of their first three albums—*Eagles, Desperado,* and *On the Border*—there is a magnificently simple recognition of the a priori desert wilderness. If you've ever lived in a desert climate, you know that grassy towns, and even the big sparkling grids of cities, do little to disguise the enormous wilderness they sit upon. It is a simple exercise to imagine the way the desert looked before the Shoshonean fluorescence, the Mormon migration, the irrigation boom, and parking lots. It's still easier to imagine it rusted over and empty someday. As the Eagles recognized, the big empty desert is waiting for the whole thing to go bankrupt. Or, as Glenn Frey coolly moans in the outlaw song "Doolin-Dalton," "The towns lay out across the dusty plains like graveyards filled with tombstones, waiting for the names."

By 1976's *One of These Nights*, the Eagles had added cocktail string arrangements, Andy Gibb-style falsetto, and the smarmy guitar of Joe Walsh. To keep pace with the increasingly shimmering sound, the Eagles pushed the myth of the West up against the rich hills of Los Angeles, culminating of course with the gaudy, poolside nervous breakdown of "Hotel California." And then it went bust, like all enterprises in the desert West do, when the parties got too big, and the water ran out.

Hotel California Club Sandwich

The bluish hotel with the mission bell towers under the palm trees catching the last roar of the sunset on the cover of 1979's Hotel California *is, as it turns out, a photograph of the super glamorous Beverly Hills Hotel whose breezy excesses are best symbolized by the hotel's California-themed club sandwich, the Sunset Club, which can be purchased poolside for $27.*

Insofar as a hotel's club sandwich is a general indicator about the nature of the hotel itself, and insofar as The Beverly Hills Hotel is the thinly disguised Hotel California, which is, in turn, the greatest riddle of rock music, I endeavor to print here, like a ciphertext, the recipe for The Beverly Hills Hotel's $27 Sunset Club.

STEP 1: MAKE THE WATERCRESS PESTO
The Sunset Club is dressed with watercress pesto, which makes the sandwich more Californian. The bitterness of the watercress is also an important counterbalance for the sweet, creamy shrimp salad. Blend a packed cup of watercress with a small clove of garlic, 1/8 cup olive oil, and a 1/2 tsp. each of salt and pepper in a food processor. Add water if necessary to reach spreadable consistency. Reserve a small handful of whole watercress to dress the sandwich.

STEP 2: MAKE THE ICEBERG COLESLAW
The Sunset Club doesn't have a leaf of deeply green lettuce laying down on it. It has a nice mat of pale and finely shredded and delicately dressed iceberg lettuce that makes the sandwich feel young and cold. Chop a quarter head of iceberg lettuce very fine. Dress lightly with 1 tsp. lemon juice and 1 tsp. vegetable oil.

STEP 3: MAKE THE COCKTAIL SHRIMP SALAD
The Sunset Club is a poolside sandwich and is designed, partly, to transport you to the ocean instead of you having to go to the ocean itself. Soak four or five saffron threads in 1 tbsp. white wine vinegar for 10 or 15 minutes, until richly colored. Remove the threads and combine the dyed vinegar with 1/8 cup mayonnaise, 1 tbsp. chopped tarragon, 1 tbsp. chopped red onion, 1 tbsp. finely diced celery, and 1/4 cup small cocktail shrimp, left whole, plus salt and pepper.

STEP 4: FRY THE BACON
Four slices of paper-thin bacon, medium done.

STEP 5: SLICE AND BRUISE THE AVOCADO & SLICE THE TOMATO
Slice the avocado into normal slices, and then mash it slightly with the back of a spoon. Then sprinkle it with the remainder of the lemon you used to dress the iceberg coleslaw. Slice the tomatoes medium thin.

STEP 6: TOAST THREE SLICES OF BREAD
I don't need to tell you a club sandwich is a club sandwich because it has three slices of bread. One of the unfortunate things about club sandwiches is this: because of their general comportment and the fact that they are served on toasted bread, they are very hard on the roof of your mouth. As such, only toast the bread on one side, using your oven broiler, keeping the soft side facing out as you assemble the sandwich. Homemade loaf-pan baked brown bread is the California sandwich standard, for its moist and soft sweetness, but any plain sliced brown bread will work.

STEP 7: ASSEMBLE THE SUNSET CLUB SANDWICH
On the bottom layer of bread spread the mashed avocado. Then arrange the paper-thin slices of bacon, and then the slices of tomato. Then put on the second layer of bread. Dress the bread with a healthy amount of the watercress pesto and top that with the whole watercress leaves. Then spread a thick layer of the shrimp salad. Pile on a large heap of the iceberg coleslaw on top of the shrimp salad, and then add the top layer of bread. You could serve it like this if you were serving it to kids or your in-laws, but to make it into a Sunset Club you would be proud to serve poolside, mash the sandwich down delicately but firmly so that it can fit in the mouths of bird-like poolside dieters, and cut off all the crusts so that—psychologically speaking—it appears to be a sandwich your own wonderful mother would set in front of you. Cut the sandwich into four triangles, and stick each triangle with a frilly toothpick that has a sun-gold cherry tomato speared onto it. The sandwich should be enjoyed with a pickle, but not with a salad. The sandwich is its own salad. You're in California by the shrimp-filled ocean after all.

PHARMAKON
Persephone

A high-concept fragrance, Persephone largely contains laboratory-engineered scent molecules that shape-shift among decomposing forbidden fruit, ions harvested from an electrical storm, musty basement, and motor speedway tire rubber. Best applied in moist creases and fleshy folds for full alchemical effect.

ARIEL PINK
Perfume Pollutant

Feel that intoxicating saccharine marshmallow smog tickling your senses? Ariel Pink's Perfume Pollutant shield provides a visible haze that grows thicker with each spray.

MAC DEMARCO
Scrambled Oeuf

Citrus overtones give way to nuanced whispers of the ashtray from a salvaged Buick, reservoir water, diner omelet, loft futon, and the crotch from the underwear left from that random girl who spent the night last night. So light it's impossible to overdose, Scrambled Oeuf is applied via trademark squirt nozzle that douses each wearer like it's halftime at club soccer playoffs.

INGREDIENTS

Watercress	1/2 tsp. pepper	1 tbsp. chopped tarragon
Bread	Head of lettuce	1 tbsp. chopped red onion
Small clove of garlic	1 tsp. vegetable oil	1 tbsp. finely diced celery
1/8 cup olive oil	1 tsp. lemon juice	1/4 cup small cocktail
1/2 tsp. salt	1/8 cup mayonaise	shrimp

TO-DO LIST
Okay, ponder these words: Proust reading group. Dads. Summer. Right?

In the Basement

In recent years, Chicago has made it almost impossible to have legitimate all-ages spaces in the city; many shows now happen in secret DIY spaces or people's houses. Here are just a few of the promoters helping keep their scenes alive and open to young fans.

**Photos by
David C. Sampson**

Kelly Nøthing, 24
Animal Kingdom

"I do it because I like DIY shows and I want them to happen. I wasn't allowed to go to club shows growing up so I went to parties and house shows—and I liked the community aspect of it."

Chris Crack, 27
New Deal
Mansion

"I just like to see people happy and having a good time. I feel like that's my job on earth. In Chicago, there are less and less house parties because of violence, because people are scared to come out. Our thing is to spread love and not charge people. They can just do what they want and have fun."

**Michael
Anthony, 28**
Them People
Studios

*"The aim is a more
communal vibe in
Chicago, and to project
it out to the world—
using our space to be
a Mecca. What we do
is grassroots, it's not
branded, so the scene
feels like it owns the
space. Our space is
Chicago's."*

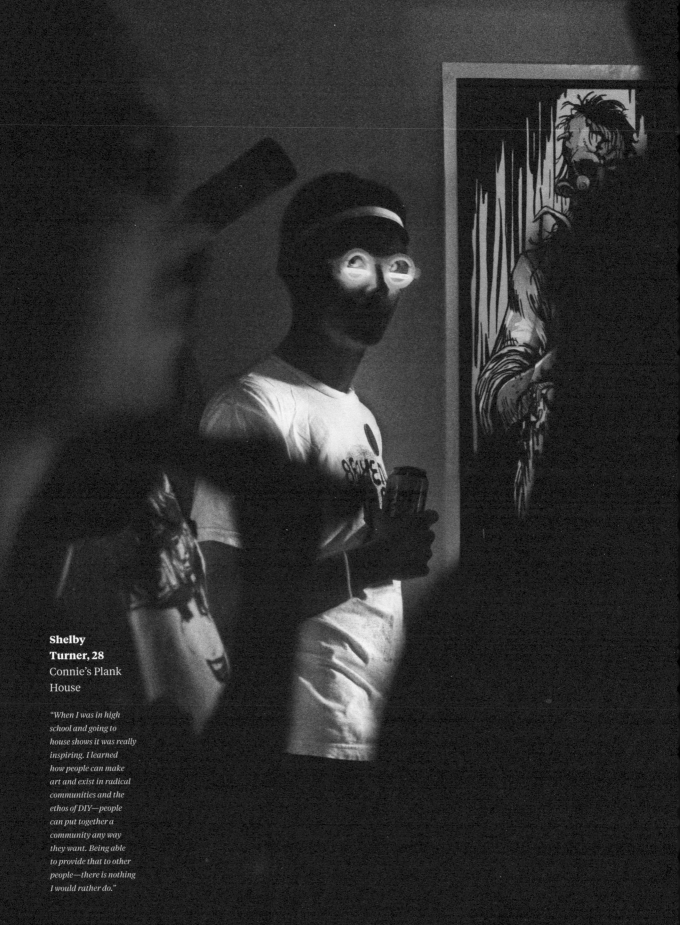

Shelby Turner, 28
Connie's Plank House

"When I was in high school and going to house shows it was really inspiring. I learned how people can make art and exist in radical communities and the ethos of DIY—people can put together a community any way they want. Being able to provide that to other people—there is nothing I would rather do."

The Passion of Jamaica's Master Trombonist Don Drummond and Margarita Mahfood, the Rhumba Queen

BLOW MY MIND

by Vivien Goldman   Illustrations by Hannah K. Lee

Tears fell on dance floors across Kingston, Jamaica, in the early hours of the first day of January 1965. Enjoying their "jump and prance" to ska, the blithe, speedy sound of independence, partygoers froze as word of the tragedy spread like wildfire from bar to nightclub. The handsome, masterful ska trombonist Don Drummond, 32, had turned himself in to the police and confessed to killing his great love, the exotic dancer, Margarita Mahfood, 25, known as the Rhumba Queen.

At that moment, every reveler who came of age with independence realized that ska would never be the same—and neither would they. The pure exuberance of ska would forever be shadowed by the eerie drumroll of innocence lost. Set to immortal dance music, Don and Margarita's passion, jealousy, betrayal, and obsessive love—not unlike a Caribbean Sid and Nancy—would never be forgotten.

As the story emerged, shocked revelers heard how Margarita, born Anita Selema Mahfood, had promised to stay home in their two-room shack at 9 Rusden Road, in Kingston's Rockfort area, and wait for Don's return from a show in the country. But the free-spirited Margarita couldn't resist partying on New Year's Eve. Returning early, Don fell prey to manic jealousy. The ensuing tragedy continues to be passionately debated up to today, much like the grim fates of John Lennon, Kurt Cobain, Tupac, and the Notorious B.I.G. Yet, oddly, Jamaica did not vilify Don Drummond for the killing, even though the gorgeous, vibrant, kind Margarita (the drop-out daughter of a prosperous Jamaican-Lebanese family) was arguably just as loved on the island. It was well known, especially in music circles, that Don was prone to "go and come in the head." He had been diagnosed with schizophrenia. Don resisted controlling his condition with drugs because they stopped him from being able to play. Knowing his own weakness, the great composer, player, and arranger, who gave us classics like "Eastern Standard Time," "Green Island," and "Man in the Street," was a withdrawn

loner, the archetype of the tortured artist capable of communicating only through his music. But nobody expected his moodiness to turn murderous.

Introverted and depressive, Don clearly benefited from Margarita's breezy, fun personality. It took a woman of Margarita's sensuality and vivacity to unlock him. Her naysayers forget that though Margarita's electric sex appeal tested Don, she, too, put up with a lot during their brief, incandescent relationship. When I discussed the relationship with Don's former bandmates, the general analysis cast Margarita as a wicked temptress responsible for Don's downfall. And that without Margarita and her flirtatious, coquettish ways, Don would still be alive, conceptualizing music to propel Jamaica into the future. But it took two to dance that fatal rhumba. Why should Margarita be blamed for her own death at the hands of a man she had loved and cared for, even when others had abandoned him?

As a founding member of one of the world's seminal house bands, Drummond's name became synonymous with The Skatalites, whom he joined in 1964. The band's name suggests the leaping optimism of the period, when a wave of nations emerged from colonialism and men walked on the moon. New frontiers were being broached on earth and in outer space.

The double tragedy struck a great blow to the newly developing Jamaican psyche. If there was extra hop in ska's bop, it came from knowing that the island, after centuries of genocide, slavery, and colonialism, was finally independent.

Like all newly emerging nations of that time, the island was conscious of its cultural capital, and the role its music played in giving the country an identity. Ska was being marketed as part of Jamaica's growing tourist industry. Yet the rhumba was still Margarita's trademark dance because of the way she shimmied during the height of the Cold War. The Berlin Wall went up in 1961, a year before Jamaican independence, and the botched Castro takedown known as the Bay of Pigs happened three years before Don joined The Skatalites in 1964.

Through the global shake-ups, Cuban music had conquered the world anyway, from the congas of *I Love Lucy*'s Desi Arnaz to the Congo. But it had a special meaning for Jamaica. As word filtered back that migrating Jamaicans were not receiving warm welcomes in their former motherland, Great Britain, there was a natural urge to seek new allies. Thus, Jamaicans placed themselves on the front lines of the Cold War, through Cuba's links with Russia. The bond between Cuba and Jamaica was as strong then as it is today. In that era, before the days of all-inclusive resorts for middle-class tourists, the Kingston waterfront was bustling with commerce. Cuban sailors were habitués of the waterfront clubs, bars, and brothels in the lost bohemian world of Rae Town, now dilapidated, where much of Don and Margarita's love played out. There, Margarita's erotic dance expressed a social reality, just as Don's plangent playing communicated the depth of the newly independent Jamaican soul.

When I first started covering Jamaican music at the source for the thriving British music press in the mid-'70s, reggae giants like Bob Marley, Gregory Isaacs, Jacob Miller, Dennis Brown, and rapping DJs known as "toast-

Don Drummond, the handsome, brooding, ska master trombonist. He created an eternal sound, but mental demons made him kill the person he loved most.

ers," such as U-Roy and Big Youth, were still active around town. In their "ganzie" cardigans and felt hats, reggae stars could be seen taking meetings with multinational record companies like Virgin or Warner Brothers. (At the time, record companies showed a spurt of interest because of "Punky Reggae Party," the musical bond between two disaffected youth subcultures, punk and Rasta.) Though they were one generation older, Don's fellow players in the legendary Skatalites—Tommy McCook, Roland Alphonso, and Jackie Mittoo—were alive and still playing. Thus, it was through his musical compadres that I first heard of Don and Margarita's turbulent story. Tommy McCook always swore Don was innocent. Musicians spoke of Don and Margarita in the present tense, as if they were still around— playing, dancing, loving, and brawling. At Don's trial, neighbors in their yard described the couple's rapport as "fighting and playing."

Both beautiful and talented, Don and Margarita became an "it" couple as soon as they got together, having met as stars of the Kingston music scene. At just 12 years old, Margarita won the famous Vere Johns' amateur show at the Ward Theatre. Still a teenager, she became a regular draw in Kingston's hectic '60s nightlife, with its elegant clubs, such as the Glass Bucket at Half Way Tree and the Club Havana on Windward Road.

Despite her success, Margarita was always friendly, genuine, and full of sparkling verve. Petite and fit, with long hair waving around her shoulders, she knew how to turn men on with her earthy energy. Her Lebanese complexion positioned her as a woman for all races. Unlike the statuesque showgirls of Havana's Tropicana Club, who inspired her flouncy, belly-baring, cha-cha-cha costumes, Margarita worked her wire-waist and did the splits on those chic

PHOTO COURTESY OF THE GLEANER COMPANY LIMITED

dance floors, just like today's twerking queens.

And that was the problem. In those more conservative times, Margarita's blessing was her curse. Her free spirit, talent, and sexy moves made her a star—but also caused her strict, abusive father (a wealthy businessman who had made his money in fish) to cast her out of their tradition-al Lebanese-Jamaican upper-middle-class family. Those magnetic hips drew Don to Margarita—but then made him ban her from dancing in public once she became his wom-an, plunging their small fam-ily unit into poverty.

When he and Margarita fell in love, Don Drummond was already a hero. *Down Beat* wrote about him, and George Shearing named him one of the world's five best trombonists. His distinctive contribution is the melancholy, searching, jazzy trombone solos that add a poignant undertow to ska's cheery gallop. Arguably, it's Don's haunt-ing, witty, sensitive solos embedded in ska's exuber-ance that give the sound its tantalizing, bittersweet flavor, suggestive of both youth and insight. That fris-son gives ska an extraordi-nary resilience, rising again and again to recharge new generations with its snappy propulsion. Ska has gone through four cycles of popularity. First, it fired up newly independent Jamai-cans, then it energized the mods and skinheads in '60s Britain. After that it inspired The Specials and other bands on 2 Tone Records in the '70s and '80s. Finally, '90s skate-punks like No Doubt (on the West Coast) and The Mighty Mighty Bosstones (on the East Coast) assumed the man-tle of ska. Now ska and its punk varieties are continuously performed—from Japan to Russia to Indonesia. But that moment in Kingston, is where it all began. In the down-town dances and plush nightclubs of an island whose rig-id color and class system was just beginning to shift and

The radiant Rhumba Queen, Margarita Mahfood. Kind heart, fit physique, and moves that set alight Kingston nightclubs—and Don Drummond's heart.

a dark-skin downtown boy could capture the heart of a light-complexioned uptown girl.

But despite their differences of class and color, Don and Margarita had much in common, as well as being leaders in their respective arts. Both headstrong and re-bellious, they each flouted the destiny dictated by their upbringing and background. It was Don's mischievous behavior—possibly shaped by early signs of his incipi-ent schizophrenia—that led his single mother, living in meager ghetto conditions, to place him with the nuns at the Alpha Boys School. Thus misfortune gave young Don a new future. The Alpha Boys School was virtually the only access to musical training for a fatherless ghetto boy. At school, his brilliance was acknowledged, but even then he was introverted and silent. He heard his own music and distrusted authority.

Before he became a key figure in The Skatalites, Don stood in an individ-ual bandshell, wearing a monogrammed jacket as part of the well-established Eric Deans swing jazz band. He was fired for hijacking the show, subverting the anticipated swing rhythms by blasting a ska solo. The crowd loved it; Deans didn't.

But Don was on a quest to find his true voice. Root-ed in African-American jazz (Don's Middle Eastern modal approach owes much to John Coltrane), his musical jour-ney was also directed by another passion he and Margar-ita shared—Rasta, the young belief system that had its own black deity in Haile Selassie, His Imperial Majesty of Ethiopia, King of Kings, Lord of Lords, Conquering Lion of the Tribe of Judah, Earth's Rightful Ruler. Many artists were among those growing dreadlocks and gravitating to the teachings, expressed in the African-derived Rasta drums and aided by smoking marijuana. Jamming with

Rasta artists like Count Ossie and the Mystic Revelation of Rastafari helped Don discover his individual artistry.

Don had always heard a different sound in his mind, one that did not always come instantly to his fellow musicians. His producer, the late Coxsone Dodd, granted me a rare interview at Studio One in Kingston. He recalled how during one session, Don was so frustrated at the other Skatalites' slowness in catching the beat that he once pulled a knife and insisted, "Who want to play, play. Who don't, leave," shocking his fellow musicians.

Coxsone Dodd's sonorous, deliberate voice had a gravitas suited to his role as reggae's elder statesman. The rhythms Dodd oversaw formed the foundation of Jamaican music recycled by artists today. Many on Studio One's roster of illustrious artists complained about their paltry remuneration; but the sheer scope of Dodd's signings tells its own story, including Bob Marley, Burning Spear, John Holt, Lee "Scratch" Perry, and most of Jamaica's great musical names. Over a decade after he'd left Studio One, Marley was still vexed about his lack of money from Dodd. Yet he would recall his times at Studio One with nostalgic affection, and call that period "an education." Don, however, never lived long enough to find that peaceful accommodation.

Assuming the financial risk, producers also assumed they would reap the bulk of any rewards. In many cases, artists were so plentiful that some regarded them as disposable. But Dodd saw the treasure he had in Don. Though Don's music was extremely popular, Dodd had a simple explanation for the money woes that beset Don. "He loved to record so much, and he had so much new music always bubbling in his mind that Don would use up his money in advance by booking studio time," the venerable Dodd explained. Of Margarita, he took a more balanced view than the other Skatalites. Even Dodd was not immune to Margarita's charms. Despite Dodd's admiration for Don, he represented what Rastafarians called Babylon, which is to say he was part of the system that thwarted and oppressed Don.

Don and Margarita were both drawn to the growing Rasta movement, whose philosophy gave meaning to their post-colonial struggle. The Rasta encampment in the Wareika Hills outside Kingston was a place of refuge for Don and Margarita. Her extraordinary talent and charisma often made her the only female dancing around the flames, while the Rastas, channeling Africa, drummed and chanted down Babylon for nights and days.

The controversial Margarita was already loved and loathed for refusing to go onstage without Rasta drummers in her set at the famous Carib Theatre. The promoters tried to resist. At that time, Rastas were outcasts, known as "blackheart men," and invoked as bogeymen to scare little kids. It was a bold move that made Margarita even more of a heroine.

Perhaps the pinnacle of Don and Margarita's great love was the Studio One session when he fulfilled her dream to record. Now readily available online, "Woman a Come" was for many years a rarity, partly because, like Margarita's musical prowess and character, the song was never taken seriously by the musical establishment. The Skatalites regarded the session as a favor to Don and as a bit of a joke. But now, Margarita's unconventional, gritty singing sounds avant-garde, a ska Yoko Ono. Despite the Rasta drums and militant womanist spirit, the song yearns with the desire of one of the most sought-after women in Kingston.

Rasta helped articulate Don's great frustration. His progressive consciousness is clear in his song titles, from "Man in the Street" to the songs that spearheaded Jamaican fascination with the Far East, like "China Town" and "Confucius." Involvement with Africa rang out on "Addis Ababa," "Marcus Junior" (referring to the son of pan-Africanist Marcus Garvey), and "The Reburial," a nod to Africa-based Pocomania rituals.

Don was a great artist, eager to progress, yet he was trapped in a rapidly changing but still deeply class- and color-conscious system. He was trapped as a musician whose creativity greatly outstripped his actual earnings. Above all, he suffered as a man trapped on his island. Because of his medical records as a schizophrenic, Don was not allowed to have a passport. The greats of America who inspired him—John Coltrane, Charlie Parker, Albert Ayler—were so tantalizingly near, but he would never get a chance to jam with them, as his talent merited. His only freedom was to blow those solos, and enjoy Margarita.

Meanwhile, Margarita's dancing had attracted attention from American impresarios. But before she was faced with the decision whether to leave Don behind and pursue a career on Broadway, she was gone.

Some of Don's peers saw Margarita as a groupie or vampire, but the emotional balance of power in their relationship seems to have been quite different. If Margarita's romantic choice files her under "women who love too much," bear in mind that her brooding superstar musician was gorgeous, but also that in falling for a man who could be difficult and rough, against the advice of her friends, she was only gravitating to what she knew. Prior to marrying Don, Margarita married and had a daughter with boxer Rudolph Bent, who allegedly batted her around a bit at home.

Margarita's father, meanwhile, never forgave her disobedience—her class betrayal—in becoming a rhumba dancer and shacking up with a broke, black, jazz musician.

Addicted to each other, neither heeded the warnings from family and friends. They were blinded by love and need. For Margarita, Don was not only a lover—he was a creative inspiration so thrilling it was worth putting up with his mood swings and recurring disappearances.

When the stress really hit, Don would disappear. Vanish. It was in this anonymous vagabond mode that Evet Hussey, my co-writer on our script, *Blow My Mind*—the phrase was a favorite of Don's—encountered him, a fleeting but poignant connection that makes an appearance in our film. As a schoolgirl, Hussey had a summer job at a resort hotel, where she befriended and fed a vagrant,

Despite their differences of class and color, Don and Margarita had much in common, as well as being leaders in their respective arts. Both headstrong and rebellious, they each flouted the destiny dictated by their upbringing and background.

against her boss' advice. After guards chased him from the property, she never thought she would see him again. But some months later, Hussey went to see The Skatalites. To her amazement, the legendary Don Drummond playing the trombone onstage was her friend, the homeless man. She never forgot how he stepped forward and played his solo, looking straight at her.

When he would reappear from one of his walkabouts, before he could rejoin his band, Don usually found himself back at an institution that would become his second home, Kingston's Bellevue Hospital for mentally ill patients.

Like New York's own psychiatric hospital of that name, Kingston's Bellevue is set on the water—but the blue Caribbean, not the gray East River. When I visited the hospital in 1985, it wasn't as grim as similar facilities. I met with psychiatrist Dr. Freddie Hickling of the University of the West Indies. When Don was in his care, Dr. Hickling was new at Bellevue, and starting to implement the arts-based treatments that led to him becoming a pariah in Jamaican psychiatric circles. Now acknowledged as a leader in his field, Dr. Hickling recently went on record as the first Jamaican psychiatrist to discredit the myth that ganja use necessarily leads to insanity.

The sympathetic Dr. Hickling showed me an astounding artifact: Don's medical history card. Scrawled in spidery capital letters were the words "GANJA INTOXIC."

The double tragedy struck a great blow to the newly developing Jamaican psyche. If there was extra hop in ska's bop, it came from knowing that the island, after centuries of genocide, slavery, and colonialism, was finally independent.

Professionals like Dr. Hickling who are knowledgeable about ganja, the healing herb, insist that people afflicted with mental disorders, such as schizophrenia, must not smoke weed. Similar to acute stress, weed can push conditions that might never have erupted into an explosion of psychosis that might vanish, recur, or remain permanent.

Dr. Hickling, Jamaica's first Rasta psychiatrist, clearly revered Don. He explained how the treatments of the early '60s were much less refined than their contemporary equivalents. Don endured crude electric shock therapy and a battery of drugs. When in Bellevue, Don was dispirited, a ghost of himself. Furthermore, regulations meant that he was not allowed to play his horn, a further erosion of his identity.

After the court case, at which Don was defended by P. J. Patterson, future Jamaican prime minister, Don was condemned to life in Bellevue instead of execution, because of his known mental condition. In previous lockdowns, Hickling told me, Don's main visitor would always be Margarita, turning up with a basket of food for her messed-up man. Those visits may have been some of Don's hardest memories as his infinite sentence stretched out before him.

But Don never served the expected years. He met his unexplained death on May 6, 1969, at 37 years old and in good physical health. There was no autopsy for the cultural giant, whom the authorities saw as a nobody who had killed a rich man's daughter. Friends at his funeral cortège kidnapped the body to examine it. But no report of wrongdoing was ever made, and his burial place is still unknown, the subject of myriad theories. So prevalent was the feeling that there was something wrong about the death of Don Drummond that his death certificate states "NO-ONE WAS CRIMINALLY RESPONSIBLE"—a curious caveat.

The riddle of Drummond's death may never be solved. Rumors started to fly. Bellevue's staff were sincere and hard-working, but their pay was never high. Was someone on the inside paid off—or was Don's death simply revenge by "haters" within Bellevue? Somehow the unlikeliest prospect of all seems to be the other suggested possibility: suicide.

As I immersed myself in Don's and Margarita's lives, I started to see hints of their doomed love in the many human exchanges around me—happily, however, without Don and Margarita's grim outcome. Still, I suddenly began to notice how we sometimes try to will those we love into being who we hope they are, and often ignore signs that they are actually quite different. Like Don and Margarita, we can betray not just our lovers, but ourselves, too. What is packed in that jumping bundle of urges and needs we call love? How much will we pay for it?

The abrupt snatching away of Don's innovative genius left a vacuum in Jamaican music that still haunts the country's jazz community. Greats who were his contemporaries, like Ernest Ranglin, Monty Alexander, Rico Rodriguez, Vin Gordon (whom they call Don Drummond Jr.), and outfits like London's Jazz Jamaica are still here to enjoy. But some will always wonder: What would Don have played had he lived?

As to our film, *Blow My Mind*, when *The Pitchfork Review* commissioned this article, we were about to shoot the trailer to raise money online, trusting in the multitudes of ska and film fans to float our boat. Encouraged by an enthusiastic response, our plan now is to bypass the trailer and go straight to producing the film. Our team presses on, bound by a shared belief that we will tell this vital story onscreen.

When Evet Hussey and I began writing *Blow My Mind*, I was angry with Don for killing that glorious woman and artist. But as the script and my understanding grew, I increasingly felt the despair and pathos behind his rage. I hope that by discovering the vulnerability behind the tumult, you, the reader, will join me in feeling only compassion for both these benighted souls, doomed to live and die for their lustrous love. ✎

Vivien Goldman is a writer, broadcaster, educator, and post-punk musician. She is the author of five books, including two on Bob Marley. An adjunct professor at NYU's Clive Davis Institute of Recorded Music, Goldman teaches courses on punk, Bob Marley, Fela Kuti, and David Bowie. Hopefully Blow My Mind, *the tale of Don and Margarita, will be on your screens soon.*

ZOLA JESUS

&

THE TEA HEADS

7 INCH SINGLE
COMING IN ISSUE 4

LIKE THE MAGNETIC BACQUET OF FRANZ ANTON MESMER OR THE ORGONE DEVICES OF WILHELM REICH ~ RON REGÉ, JR.'S

CYMATIC THEREMAPY

ATTEMPTS TO ILLUSTRATE OUR ABILITY TO TRANSFORM THE STRUCTURE OF MATTER THROUGH SUBTLE SHIFTS OF VIBRATION.

(THE EARLY ELECTRONIC INSTRUMENT THAT IS PLAYED WITHOUT TOUCHING IT.)

THEY CALL IT "OOBLECK"

WHEN YOU MIX

WATER & CORN STARCH

THEREMIN

AMP?

SPEAKER

PLASTIC WRAP
food coloring

(optional)

DISRUPTIONS TO THE ELECTRICAL RADIO FIELD OF THE THEREMIN CAUSES FORMS AND PATTERNS TO EMERGE IN LIQUIDS PLACED IN A MAGNETIC SPEAKER CONE.

← frequency (pitch) *
* volume

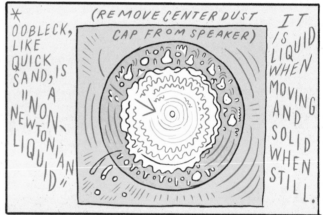

* OOBLECK, LIKE QUICKSAND, IS A "NON-NEWTONIAN LIQUID"

(REMOVE CENTER DUST CAP FROM SPEAKER)

IT IS LIQUID WHEN MOVING AND SOLID WHEN STILL.

THIS DISPLAY ILLUSTRATES THE FLUCTUATION OF ELECTRIC AND MAGNETIC VIBRATION THAT EXISTS WITHIN EVERYTHING & EFFECTS THE STRUCTURE OF ALL MATTER.

* IT IS ALSO INSPIRED BY THE SPIRITUAL POWER BATTERY OF THE AETHERIUS SOCIETY.

PLAYING THE THEREMIN IS LIKE TAI-CHI. AFTER A WHILE YOU REALLY START TO FEEL THE ELECTRIC FIELDS.

THE MYSTERIOUS CONTENTS OF OUR OWN THOUGHTS & EMOTIONS OPERATE ON THESE SAME PRINCIPLES OF FLUCTUATING VIBRATION.

LIKE THE SHIFTING CYMATIC PATTERNS IN A DROP OF WATER, OUR MINDS BOTH CREATE & ARE EFFECTED BY THE VIBRATIONS SURROUNDING US.

CYMATIC THEREMAPY IS A VISUAL REMINDER THAT OUR EXISTENCE IS NOT LIKE A SHIP CAST OUT ON A SEA OF STATIC. OUR MINDS POSSES THE ABILITY TO CREATE AND TRANSFORM AN INFINITE VARIATIONS OF VIBRATING FORMS.

THE STRUCTURE OF ALL MATTER ON EARTH, OUR FLOATING SPECK OF DUST & WATER, CAN BE TRANSFORMED INSTANTLY BY THE SLIGHTEST SHIFT OF VIBRATION. ～ ALL CONSCIOUSNESS IS UNIFIED IN THIS CREATION ～

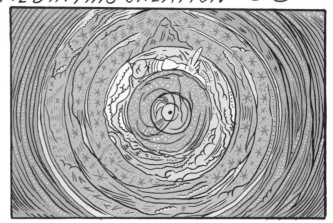

WE CONTRIBUTE BOTH AS ISOLATED INDIVIDUALS AND AS A UNIFIED WHOLE.

ANYTHING WE IMAGINE CAN BE CREATED IN PHYSICAL FORM.

① "THE IMPLODING VORTEX"

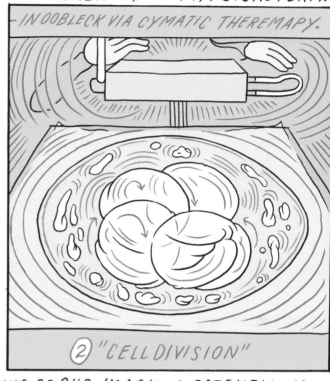

② "CELL DIVISION"

THE ONLY BARRIER TO THE UNLEASHING OF OUR IMAGINED POTENTIAL IS THE ISOLATING SENSATION OF FEAR. ALL WE EXPERIENCE IS A VARIATION OF ONE VIBRATION.

③ "HEAD AND SHOULDERS"

④ "THE WRITHING SNAKE"

THE ANSWER IS LOVE.

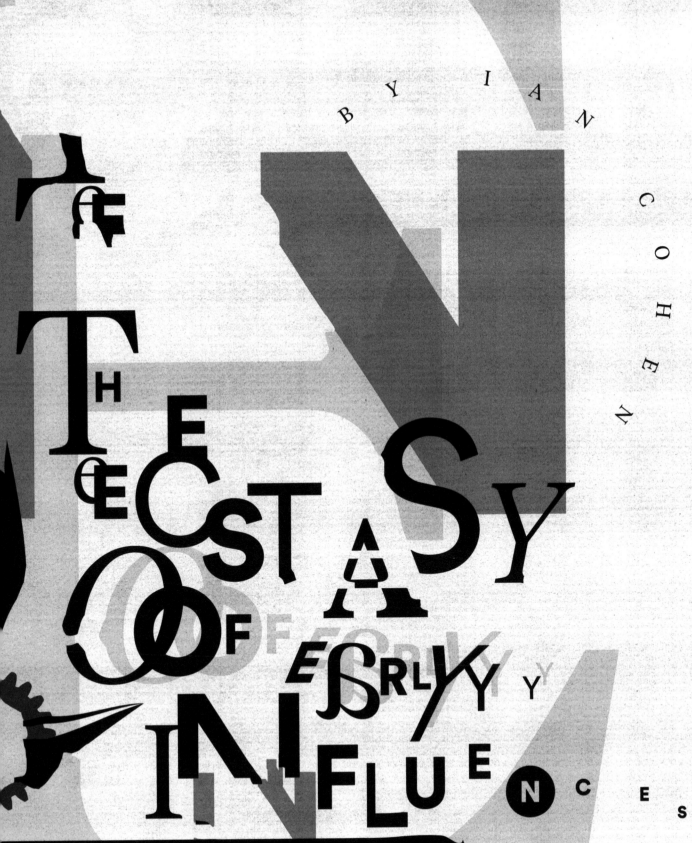

BY IAN COHEN

THE ECSTASY OF EARLY INFLUENCES

REVISITING YOUTHFUL INDISCRETIONS

Kids these days can't innocently engage with music without some adult opening his big, fat mouth. It's something Hazel Cills addressed in an article published in *Rookie* earlier this year. In "Kids Won't Listen," Cills took issue with "articles about teenage girls written by grown-up men." Or to be more specific, music presumed to be consumed exclusively by teenage girls.

The article included a tirade against Jody Rosen, who had profiled Taylor Swift for *New York* magazine. It mattered not that Rosen's piece was in depth, sensitively written, and curious, or that Swift endorsed it and would probably be insulted by the regressive idea that only people in an age demographic a decade younger than she is can relate to her music. The point was that Rosen was overstepping his bounds simply by not being a teenage girl.

Months later, Saul Austerlitz of the *New York Times Magazine* had a similarly flawed argument in "The Pernicious Rise of Poptimism." He made some valid points: that coverage of pop tends to border on celebrity worship, and that those who don't toe the party line on Beyoncé get bullied by other critics, which was proven the moment it was published. Those points, however, were marred by completely indefensible ideas about The National being overlooked by critics, and how Haim is somehow responsible for latter-day Strokes albums not getting a fair shake. My ears started steaming by the second paragraph. And yet, by coming from completely opposite directions, Cills and Austerlitz made the same point: adults have no business trying to think about music like a 13-year-old.

Cills and Austerlitz write as if one day you're in middle school, listening to Drake and Taylor Swift, and then snap! twenty years pass, and you're listening to The National and Speedy Ortiz. Both writers completely skip over alternative rock—the introductions, the crossovers, the point

where you have to take a leap of faith into a place you may live to regret if you hang around the cool kids. The battle here isn't between pop and indie rock—they're portrayed as part of the same continuum. Instead, it's alternative rock against indie rock. And that's a big deal because the latter seems put in place to make the former feel like complete dog shit.

Sadie Dupuis, frontwoman of the angular, acerbic Speedy Ortiz, raved about deep cuts from the Toadies' *Rubberneck*, an album that celebrates its 20th anniversary this summer with a deluxe reissue and sold out shows at the Troubadour in Los Angeles. Meanwhile, three of the most unique, challenging male singer-songwriters in indie rock—Devon Walsh of Majical Cloudz, Tom Krell of How to Dress Well, and Alex Zhang Hungtai of Dirty Beaches—engaged in a lengthy Twitter discussion about the genius of the gnomic, guyliner'd poetry Chino Moreno penned in Deftones. It culminated in Walsh posting a performance of "Back to School (Mini Maggit)," a bonus track tacked onto deluxe editions of *White Pony*, intended to capitalize on the rap-metal surge the Deftones clearly weren't a part of. (In the video, Moreno jumps on lunch tables and raps about drinking vodka: a nu-metal, bro'd out rendering of *Never Been Kissed*.) At Brooklyn DIY venue 285 Kent's closing party, a DJ played the title track from System of a Down's *Toxicity*, which caused the audience of twentysomethings to, by all accounts, lose their shit.

What exactly is happening here, other than hip indie

types embracing the music of their youth? There's no danger of these '90s alt-rock bands becoming an intentional or even an ironic influence. It's as harmless as karaoke. In contrast to the Backstreet Boys or Nelly or any other pop from that time, you'll never see a poptimist embrace of the Toadies or Deftones. And yet Ben Greenberg has a huge fucking problem with this.

Greenberg is one of three guitarists and singers in The Men, a New York indie rock band beholden to their formative listening experiences. You think he'd be able to appreciate people tapping into the sheer joy music once brought them, but The Men's record collection is alt-rock free: experimental Sonic Youth, Swans, and every dirty, grim New York City indie act that never came close to a DGC deal. True, they've gotten into Zep and Skynyrd, but when you do that sort of thing late in your career, the assumption is that you've learned to listen to them correctly. You skipped over that *Hammer of the Gods* shit and had nary a bong rip in the blacklight glow of your friend's basement.

Greenberg's problem with System of a Down has everything to do with Perfect Pussy, a blazingly feminist, no-fi punk band that's never sounded anything like "Chop Suey!" In a review of Perfect Pussy's much-buzzed *Say Yes to Love* for artist-on-artist site *The Talkhouse*, Greenberg lays out legitimate issues with the record: it lacks proper "songs"; the straight-to-tape recording is an affectation; the last eight minutes of a 23-minute record is ambient drone. Greenberg makes it pretty clear Perfect Pussy is focused more on capitalizing on their buzz than turning in the strongest, most thought-out record possible.

But he's also got an axe to grind. Greenberg says Perfect Pussy's sonic assault is tantamount to what happened at 285 Kent. "Hearing a System of a Down song blast over the PA presses another brain-button to remind you that

yes, you did sit around your suburban basement and try to find drugs when you were in high school." And here's the money quote: "Were you having a sincere reaction to the content of the music, or were you just yukking it up and rolling with the sonic moment?" What I got out of this isn't that Greenberg has a problem with System of a Down or even with Perfect Pussy. Replace those two bands with Slipknot and Deafheaven. You get the same argument shared by many in his position: he's criticizing the way teenagers interact with rock music. More to the point, he's criticizing teenagers for not knowing exactly who they want to be.

All of a sudden, I feel this innate sense of protectiveness, like a lion with its cub, except my cub is Serj Tankian or *Pinkerton* or something. There's criticism and then there's the handing down of judgment on a person in a helpless emotional state. Hell, I remember most of my first experiences with music criticism being like, "Yeah, what you're listening to sucks, don't you get it?" And it was a message conveyed by someone older and presumably cooler than I was.

But I'm also aware that one of music criticism's most pernicious and wrongheaded threads is the one that assumes a teen's listening habits are *superior* to an adult's. This is predicated on the idea that adults listen to music because of context, cred-consciousness, and anything but "rolling with the sonic moment." When I interviewed Chris Mojan of mature pop-punk band Fireworks, he summed up what it's like to have a younger fanbase: they're excited to see a band, to be part of something for the first time. Now, I don't know if I'd stretch so far as to say that 13-year-olds listen to music without much regard for what's cool. In fact, nothing means more to a typical teen than being cool or accepted.

We can discuss this binary further by identifying a lit-

> I'm also **aware that one of music criticism's most pernicious and wrongheaded threads is the one that assumes a teen's** listening **habits are superior to an adult's. This is predicated on the idea that adults listen to music because of context, cred-consciousness, and everything but** "rolling **with the sonic moment."**

eral personification of it: Billy Corgan vs. Steve Malkmus. The funny thing about this rivalry is that both feel like it's a completely unfair fight, and the other guy has the upper hand. Critics and fans of The Smashing Pumpkins agree the band's mindset—really Billy Corgan's—is stuck in a perpetual state of high school junior-ism. A large part of this is blowing everything out of proportion. The fact that Corgan has taken every opportunity to rekindle a grudge inspired by a 1994 Pavement lyric should be proof enough. The following line probably shouldn't be at the center of a beef spanning two decades: "Out on tour with The Smashing Pumpkins / Nature kids, I / They don't have no function / I don't understand what they mean / And I could really give a fuck." It stings, but not exactly.

Why should Billy Corgan give a shit about what Pavement thought about him? The Smashing Pumpkins ruled the '90s in just about every measurable metric. *Siamese Dream* is four times platinum and is included on almost every greatest albums list (though always lower than *Slanted and Enchanted*). *Pisces Iscariot* debuted at number four on Billboard—and it's a B-sides collection. *Mellon Collie and the Infinite Sadness* is certified diamond and spawned approximately 15 videos, each with a budget probably exceeding the total recording cost of Pavement's discography. Corgan is rich beyond his wildest dreams, unless his wildest dreams involve owning a professional wrestling league and playing eight-hour synth jams based on *Siddhartha* at a tea house he opened in the Chicago suburbs. (In that case, he's exactly as rich as his wildest dreams.)

But consider the substance behind Malkmus' taunts. For one thing, Steve Albini thought The Smashing Pumpkins were a bunch of phonies, or at least "careerists." In 1993, I did not know who Steve Albini was—what I did know is that, while I appreciated the drums on "Scentless Apprentice," I didn't think *In Utero* was anywhere near as good as *Nevermind*. It sounded like a talented band making a concerted effort to be less popular, a concept I had no ability to grasp in the seventh grade.

I'd find out later that Steve Albini wasn't the only person in Chicago who found The Smashing Pumpkins to be a bunch of careerists; nor were The Smashing Pumpkins the only Chicago band Albini took umbrage at. There was also Urge Overkill, a band whose major-label debut *Saturation* I adored so much that I bought a miniature UO medallion and a T-shirt at the first concert I ever attended. I wore it to school one day, and was promptly mocked because who the fuck was Urge Overkill? "Sister Havana"

wasn't exactly getting "No Rain" spins on MTV. As far as I was concerned, *Saturation* was the epitome of outsider rock. My brother and I pooled our money to purchase their Touch and Go predecessor *The Supersonic Storybook*. But it sounded flat and dull—no hooks, no swagger, nothing that would make me put myself on the line. Why would anyone prefer that?

There are surely other considerations: The Smashing Pumpkins were a fake indie band, releasing *Gish* on Caroline, a shell label for the eventual call up to Virgin, Caroline's parent company. And Billy Corgan seems to be obsessed with not being cool and really fucking pissed about it. While all of this vitriol should make me loathe The Smashing Pumpkins, it actually makes me like them more. It demonstrates the mind-meld Corgan could have with his fans. One bad day in gym class and it's like the entire school is against you. One insult by Pavement and it's like the entirety of Chicago and the indie rock scene really, *really* hates you.

Have you listened to "Cherub Rock" lately, the first song on *Siamese Dream*? It turns out what drove Corgan to a near mental breakdown was trying to sort out scene politics in a place nicknamed Drag City: "Stay cool / And be somebody's fool this year ... Hipsters unite / Come align for the big fight to rock for you." Billy Corgan was not cool. He *is* not cool. Here he is in his own words from a 2012 *Stereogum* interview:

> It's easy to pick on the geek. They didn't pick on Kurt because they all wanted to be Kurt. They all wanted to be Beck, they all want to be Thom Yorke. Thom Yorke's okay because he's "the right look" funny. I'm not "the right look" funny. I'm six-four, I've got my mother's hips, people are like, "Who is this guy?" I wouldn't be up there if I weren't talented, you know? And music saved my life. Music is a sacred thing to me, and I jump up and down about it, get silly about it, but I obviously have a holy reverence for it.

So when he said Malkmus "made him a target" the way a high school bully does, it had nothing to do with brawn. (Rumor has it Billy can dunk a basketball.) It's because Pavement represented everything out of reach for a guy like Corgan. Malkmus represented adulthood, or at least college—surrounded by peers of his own choosing. He didn't really care, and yet it worked out anyway. There was something confident about Pavement, despite their

ILLUSTRATION BY SAM TAYLOR

^
IAN COHEN AT HIS BAR MITZVAH, 1993.

No matter how clueless I was in navigating Plymouth-Whitemarsh High School's social strata, the common ground of alt-rock allowed me to fake it until I graduated.

slacker reputation. As long as the people who determine the canon are well-educated white guys who eke out an honest living, Pavement will keep winning, as they do to this day.

I respect people my age who were listening to Yo La Tengo or Pavement in the mid-'90s. That shit took effort, like reading *SPIN* instead of *Rolling Stone*, or staying up late to watch *120 Minutes* on MTV, or simply endearing yourself to an older or cooler crowd. I often wonder whether I'd have been better off if some magical older brother figure (as opposed to my *actual* older brother) surreptitiously swapped my Red Hot Chili Peppers album with a Red House Painters CD? What if I had heard actual Fugazi and Black Flag albums as opposed to seeing their names scrawled into desks and assuming they were the province of kids who weren't taking AP classes?

Probably nothing. I've come to appreciate those bands later in life. As an overweight, sheltered kid whose understanding of the world was limited to standardized testing and *Bulls versus Blazers* (on Sega only), I didn't need help finding ways to separate myself from my peers. God bless the kids who knew right away that being an outcast or a punk rocker was something that would determine the trajectory of their life. But once again, don't blame a teen because they're not ready to put themselves in a position to be humiliated or ostracized when finding a prom date or a couple like-minded people to sit with during a football game.

Making friends was relatively easy up to the sixth grade. You hung out with kids within walking distance of your house. You were set up with your parents' friends' kids. You played basketball or rough-touch football. You played Nintendo. You traded baseball cards. In all, your options were extremely limited. But once you started to develop a sense of self, to know who your people were, when CompuServe or Prodigy teased the freedom that AOL chat rooms would bring, things changed. Knowing a certain kind of music was there for you. You didn't hear it on the school bus. It wasn't a clear extension of the music heard in your parents' car. You weren't going to find the VFW shows or the other forums of legitimate punk rock experience if you didn't know at least someone who might know some people who knew some people.

And in that sense, alternative rock offered a legitimate alternative to a suburban kid who had no options besides MTV, the radio, and the occasional issue of *Rolling Stone*. Alternative rock was a comforting nudge toward the fringe while you figured out how to make the honor roll and not be grounded when time came for the school trip to Hershey Park. I can connect The Cure to Depeche Mode to The Smashing Pumpkins to Deftones to AFI to My Chemical Romance. Their albums allow you to think of yourself in three different, interrelated ways: kinda dark, kinda sensitive, but certainly popular in spite of everything.

No matter how clueless I was in navigating Plymouth-Whitemarsh High School's social strata, the common ground of alt-rock allowed me to fake it until I graduated.

In 2014, bands don't have to be accountable for a mass audience the way they used to, nor do listeners have to be a captive audience.

But years later when it came time to assemble "The Top 200 Tracks of the 1990s" feature at *Pitchfork*, I learned that, crass as it sounds, Nirvana was the only band to really survive the alt-rock gold rush.

My original number two choice was a rueful, profoundly sad, dark comedy of an alt-rock hit written by an addict who took his own life in exile. I don't think anybody remembers where they were when "Hey Jealousy" songwriter Doug Hopkins (then booted from The Gin Blossoms) committed suicide. His demons weren't present in the music, which somehow makes it even more startling than, say, "All Apologies." My number one pick was Foo Fighters' "Everlong," a song written by Nirvana's drummer who later embraced the corporate rock machine, who didn't say a bunch of cool things about K Records or injure himself by tossing his bass in the air during the VMAs. "Everlong" galvanized an entire genre and ensured Gil Norton's blinding production glare on *The Colour and the Shape* would determine the course of modern rock more than his work with the Pixies.

It was a culmination of hard truths learned throughout my late teens and 20s. Nine Inch Nails were just ripping off artists on the famed industrial Wax Trax! label. Wee-

zer were misogynist pseudo-geeks. Even motherfucking *Kid A* was derivative. And yet, through it all, I never really learned why Ira Kaplan's or J Mascis' guitar playing was actually more interesting than Dean DeLeo's—have you seen a Stone Temple Pilots guitar tablature? What made Gin Blossoms or Goo Goo Dolls inherently inferior to latter-day Replacements? Didn't Rancid put kids in a position to eventually discover The Clash?

Which brings us back to Greenberg's original point. Maybe he really does think it's possible for a teenager to mindlessly engage with Perfect Pussy without being aware of their personal politics. But even if people are listening to Perfect Pussy in the wrong way, as it were, isn't that progress? Or at least a shorter distance to a record by The Men than, say, Cage the Elephant? Who wouldn't want a teenager to learn about gender relations from "Interference Fits" as opposed to, say, "Sex Type Thing"? Isn't it great that a teenage pop star like Lorde can serve as an entry point to Broken Social Scene rather than a distraction or a barrier to them? When I see a 14-year-old at Coachella or the Pitchfork Music Festival, I can't tell whether I envy them. Does DIIV or St. Vincent give them the ammunition to fight against the eternal scourge of teen angst, which will *always* outgun them? How awesome is it that bands billed in the smallest font are Waxahatchee and Courtney Barnett, not G. Love & Special Sauce or Sons of Elvis? We may not need alt-rock anymore—but if it's going to soldier on in the form of bands like Foster the People, what's wrong with that?

In my mind, the problem is an underlying guilt I think most critics feel—it relates to the way they listen to music. In short, they're more embarrassed by what they were listening to at 25 than at 15. My list for "The 50 Best Albums of 2008" stands up to way less scrutiny than my list from 1994, a year I might not have even heard 50 albums in their entirety. After all, teens didn't coin "chillwave," "French touch," or "witch house," nor are they responsible for The Hold Steady. It makes me feel like Adam Silver trying to justify the NBA's minimum age limit: Kids need time to make mistakes, and it shouldn't be on our watch!

And yet, I feel like my favorite rock records of the past decade learned things from alt-rock, or at least made a conceptual link to show a deep, deep respect for the way teenagers engage with rock music—which is to say they have ambitions to be loved on a massive scale, without much of an idea of how to be cool about it. The records are theatrical and role-playing in a manner that Black Keys, Kings of Leon, White Stripes, and Queens of the Stone Age sorely lack. And really, any sort of respect they get from an older generation feels completely unintentional. I envy anyone who was 16 or so when Titus Andronicus' *The Monitor* dropped, since it shares Billy Corgan's sense of persecution and his propensity to blow shit way out of proportion. Patrick Stickles had a bad run at college, and it parallels the Civil War. The last song is 16 minutes and has a bagpipe solo to boot. And while "You will always be a loser / And that's okay" doesn't quite align with "Despite all my rage I am still just a rat in a cage," it still gives the listener a choice. It's either empowerment or confirmation that everyone is pretty fucked, especially if you're more at risk for a swirlie than the average guy.

M83's Anthony Gonzalez is an avowed Smashing Pumpkins fan. His 2011 commercial breakthrough *Hurry Up, We're Dreaming* is consciously modeled after *Mellon Collie and the Infinite Sadness*. It's a double album, despite the fact that it's barely over 75 minutes. This guy gets it: the operatic scope, the lavish production, the obsession with antiquated, almost completely non-sexual romance. Deerhunter's *Halcyon Digest* could easily have

been an oddball '90s hit along the lines of *Last Splash* or *The Bends* or *Transmissions from the Satellite Heart*, if it had a quirky Spike Jonze or Stéphane Sednaoui video to go with it.

So what's wrong with outcasts having a forum to get rich and feel like part of the in crowd? Alt-rock radio was some sneaky shit. In a weird way, it's the most gentle indie rock indoctrination possible. I heard Belly before I knew who the Breeders were. I heard Breeders before I knew the Pixies existed. An hour of alt-rock radio programming may have included Meat Puppets, Dinosaur Jr., Breeders, Sonic Youth, Hole, Björk, and Soundgarden—bands with unimpeachable, gnarled indie roots, yet they had gold and platinum plaques celebrating sales milestones for the recording industry. You could also hear undeniably just-off bands like Live or Better Than Ezra or, ahem, "Creep" and realize that some of the most homogenized radio filler can result in great songs that will unify you and your peers in 20 years.

In 2014, bands don't have to be accountable for a mass audience the way they used to, nor do listeners have to be a captive audience. If you like Japandroids, you don't have to hear an Imagine Dragons song if you don't want to. Haim fans can avoid The 1975. You might as well consider Frank Ocean or Haim today's alt artists, tapping into the insider-outsider dynamic without giving themselves over to the blind rage and confusion of puberty. It's comforting.

Sure, maybe it's still a pain in the ass to like Falling in Reverse or The Wonder Years when they're playing Drake at school dances. Today you can go home and find your people on Facebook or Twitter or Instagram. Is it any wonder Billy Corgan is in such a pissy mood these days? When he looks at the people who might've been his fans in 2014, he sees a bunch of secure, plugged-in kids with options. Kids who don't need unifiers, who can listen to The Smashing Pumpkins and their ilk and just say, #theydonthavenofunction. ✎

Ian Cohen is a contributing editor at Pitchfork and favorably reviewed System of a Down's Toxicity for his college newspaper. However, the grade was lowered from an A- to a B+ because the editor didn't think it was as good as a Tori Amos covers album. He currently lives in Los Angeles and hasn't seen any of Serj Tankian's art installations.

Burgerland

BY DYLAN TUPPER RUPERT

Photograph by Cali Thornhill DeWitt

Disneyland is not just a children's fantasyland; it's a place you visit forever. It's a space of not just cultural but psychic influence for kids who grew up in the blue-sky tracts of SoCal suburbia around Anaheim and heard the Disneyland fireworks every night as they went to sleep. Disneyland's long shadow fostered a culture of young dreamers now opting for Neverland fantasy and possibilities borne of a pop culture kingdom, in lieu of a conventional adulthood.

From the Shelves of Burger Records

BRGR089 AUDACITY –
MELLOW CRUISERS [LP]

Original snotty Burger suburba-punk boys from the garages/backyard swimming pools of Orange County. This follow-up to their first release, *Power Drowning*, is a zippy, 30-minute ripper clean enough to satisfy a power-pop craving but as playful, careless, and gruff as their crunchy, no-fucks teenage debut.

BRGR012 NOBUNNY –
RAW ROMANCE [CASS/CD/LP]

Our caricatured hero of gutter pop becomes an instant classic and bona fide star of Burger with *Raw Romance*. This Oakland underground animorph of national notoriety dishes up scratchy, strummy, already-been-chewed bubble-gum jams that are sugary sweet at first but, after you pay a little more attention, not quite so squeaky clean at all.

BRGR269 KING TUFF – S/T [CASS]

He's a cartoon troll in a leather jacket, a wild-eyed battery pack of charisma and charm. Package this all up in one of Burger's most anticipated releases after their success re-pressing his 2008 underground success, *Was Dead*, King Tuff delivers catchy, maximum-impact boppers and glistening-pop melodies strung through layers of his nasally coo and shredding riffs that particularly shine on tracks "Alone & Stoned" and "Bad Thing."

It might seem questionable why Burger Records is being built inside the strip-mall landscape of Fullerton, California. It's a place seemingly devoid of anything inspiring, yet here, Burger Records is fomenting what could be called a movement. What began in 2007 as a way for founders Sean Bohrman and Lee Rickard to self-release the recordings of their band, Thee Makeout Party!, quickly grew into a standby for those hungry for what was happening in Californian underground rock. They put out their first cassettes in 2008, and, with co-owner Brian Flores, opened the Burger headquarters and retail store in 2009 on 645 S. State Blvd. in Fullerton, just a few miles away from where they all grew up. Brian manages store operations, while Sean and Lee direct and develop the label and culture of Burger.

The Burger team is day-and-night, weekends-and-holidays occupied with building a kingdom high from the buzz of youthful enthusiasm and positive energy that thrives around their artists and their ethos. Sean and Lee are certainly unconventional cultural engineers—"imagineers," I'm tempted to claim, like an underground Walt and Roy—creating an empire they tout hyperbolically as "a philanthropic, quasi-religious, borderline-cultish, propaganda-spreading group of suburban perma-teen mutants." This crew and this scene is full of the faithful—believers in the eternity of youth and the immortality of rock and roll, and the Disney-like mantra of following your dreams. The maxim is lived by the Burger masterminds themselves. They run on bong rips and fast food, van exhaust and tour exhaustion, and all the hallmarks of dedication that mark a true lifer, because there's certainly no other life for them. There is no rest for those who run Burger Records, where the narrative of rock and roll is not being simply retold, but lived in all its grunge and glory.

With Burger there's so much for fans to grab onto. They've released 700 tapes and more than 100 vinyl LPs. The shop has become a Mecca for both touring bands and dedicated fans, packed with bins of vintage LPs and wobbling towers of VHS cassettes alongside new, shrink-wrapped Burger releases. Burger is savvy with their bubblegum marketing, which gives their entire product, from music to merchandise, a collect-'em-all appeal. Go to a Burger show and see their signature "I'm a Burger Girl/Boy/Babe/Alien/Freak/Head/Bopper" three-inch round buttons in Cooper Black font, bright colors, and the Burger logo Lee drew adorning the denim jackets and backpacks of the dearly devoted. They're huge, goofy badges of belonging for those bold enough to claim the movement as their own.

Embedded in the sprawling freeways and newness that mark the landscape of Southern California are narratives of stardom, rock 'n' roll, the American dream, and a century's worth of visions of sun-drenched salvation. The landscape permits all flights of upward mobility: it can provide the all-American autonomist with suburban comforts and the subcultural weirdo her very own space to bake in the sun. It can give the permanent child a place to go; for many

Co-founder Sean Bohrman at his usual spot in the back of Burger Records, where he also lives.

imaginations, it's a playground. Perhaps the reason such individualities can co-exist in Southern Californian culture is because there's just that much space.

The very manufacture of a landscape both geographically and culturally oriented toward expanse, comfort, and entertainment—from Hollywood to Huntington Beach with six-laned expressways in between—grants wide berth to dreamers who thrive in defying what was engineered for them, this monotony of paved-over orange groves. A certain cultural sterility settled in sometime after the sandy romance of Hawthorne's Beach Boys but before the hardcore counterblast of Hermosa Beach's Black Flag. These suburbs breed boredom, and dreaming is merely coping with the doldrums inherent. Rock 'n' roll is the most alluring remnant of midcentury American dreaming, and the most available to twenty-first-century kicks-seeking teenagers.

The critic Greil Marcus suggests that rock 'n' roll is "a story you can become part of, that can situate you precisely where history and legends collide, can help you perhaps to define your own place in your society, or outside of it." It's these dialogues, the flirtation between the legend and the new, that give this Burger happening its spark of magic and mythos. Part of the thrill is to witness their own chapter getting written. If there's any trace of nostalgia in the Burger school's bleached-out jangles and aggravated crunches of fuzz slipping out from the cracks of a cul-de-sac garage, it is, like all ensuing rock and roll efforts by default of their origins, a reprise of what was written before all of this—this rock 'n' roll story that is nothing new but everything special.

This rock 'n' roll mythology is a history of cultural dreaming in color and sound. For Burger Records, it is being staged in this land of artificial magic, but magic nonetheless, and it's the kind of dreaming that sparks wild why-not ambition. It's Californian, almost cartoon-like in its romantic caricature of the landscape and its personalities. It's born from a collective imagination that, as ambassador to the Californian psyche Joan Didion describes, "remains obdurately symbolic, tending to locate lessons in what the rest of the country perceives only as scenery." It's this asphalt that paves the way to a cultural Neverland, a place where never growing up seems to be a credible decision, a challenge of choice that those who run the Burger empire have attacked with an endearing

PHOTOGRAPH BY STEELE O'NEAL

BRGR301 THE MEMORIES –
LOVE IS THE LAW [CASS/LP]
Syrupy stoner teenage basement romantics trip on the border of novelty and endearment with breezy love songs to all manners weed and women and doing stupid shit with your friends. Micro-treasures like "Higher" and "Go Down on You" set the tone, while goofy tracks à la "Like Rikker" remind you of the dumb-boy universe they hail from. The keystone act of Gnar Tapes, Burger's slacker brigade of soul brothers from Portland, Oregon, is low on gloss and pretension and high on, well, drugs, but their pop prescription is easy and addictive.

BRGR520 CHERRY GLAZERR –
HAXEL PRINCESS [CASS/CD/LP]
Effortlessly cool teen girl anthems and after-school gems from one of Burger's youngest groups, Cherry Glazerr. Think perfectly unpolished soundtracks to all the most special bits of adolescent tedium, spelled out in titles like "Teenage Girl," "Bloody Bandaid," and "Grilled Cheese," where singer Clem Creevy's low-key, lighthearted vocals and charming humor slip out of what sounds like the smirking grin of a kid just having fun.

BRGR497 COSMONAUTS –
PERSONA NON GRATA [CASS/CD/LP]
There's that fuzzed-out trail well trodden by the likes of The Jesus and Mary Chain and The Brian Jonestown Massacre, and Cosmonauts are deadpan as they shuffle down that same one set by their shoegazing heroes. One of Burger's more sonically sophisticated releases keeps the angst on regardless, dishing up an appealingly resolved psych/shoegaze bent with their consistent atmosphere of cool kid blasé.

BRGR666 KIM FOWLEY –
LET'S GET BLASTED [CASS]
With Kim Fowley's adamant approval, Burger cements itself in the weirdo chapter of Southern Californian rock history with the release of a (fragile) living legend. The Hollywood freak-pop veteran provides the youth of today with a whirling, weird dose of ominous advice ("You Won't be Young Forever," "Your Computer is Slowly Killing You"), packed in one strange pill of spoken word and skewed-up distortion. This, to Burger, is what working with your heroes looks like.

Gabe Fulvimar of Gap Dream in the parking lot at Burger. He lives there, too. You have to go outside to smoke cigarettes.

Burger Patty's hands. She's the president of the Memories Fan Club.

energy that seems to never tap out, because this is not just a full-time dream, but an overtime operation.

In an era of American history void of a true counter-culture, Sean and Lee of Burger Records foster a subculture built on some of the same foundations of the more cheerful lessons of the '60s. Rock 'n' roll is at once a series of life choices, but also a story exploded with the stuff of myth: heroes, tragedies, runaways, triumph. It's the text that the dreamers want to be a part of; all movements have a plotline, and the rock and roll ones have the most vibrant characters, and no one is ever drafting the ending.

Burgerama: a two-day, three-stage fest at The Observatory in Santa Ana that sold out to 3,000 heads (mostly pastel-dyed, crowd-surfing teenage ones). Burgerama is California rock 'n' roll youth culture at its peak, promoting the same thrill of recreational transcendence one might look for just nine miles away in Anaheim.

The Observatory hides between office parks and fast food chains, behind an unassuming corner of Harbor Boulevard, which takes you to the eastern edge of the Disneyland fortress. Continue north for five miles, and you arrive in Fullerton, one right turn and you're walking distance from Burger Records headquarters. These main drags are more than congested soul-sucks of traffic and suburban drudgery. They're the veins through which the blood of this scene will drive through, for hours, in traffic, usually coming from their parents' house, to pulse youthful energy into these spaces of magical happening obscured between expanses of beige overdevelopment and charmless expanse. And these kids in their cars are driving this scene forward into its moment, where Burger has every intention to stay forever.

It's gatherings like Burgerama—and, for that matter, Oakland's sister fest Burger Boogaloo, or their SXSW party Burgermania—that underscore this scene's authentic moment. Those representatives who make it happen— those are the ones who all come as participants in the Burger uprising, with the conviction that this is an event to be a part of. It's conviction that creates the story, and the story that gets picked up and thrown into the cycle of youthful, subcultural consciousness.

My friend, who goes by Burger Patty, tells me that once she got her Disneyland season pass and started taking regular solo trips, she'd stop by Burger Records on the way to pick up new tapes from bands she'd never heard before. Part of the low-risk logic behind releasing cassettes in 2014 is that pricing a tape by an unknown band at $6 isn't too big of a gamble for a new listener, and most beaters that kids or bands would be driving are cassette compatible. The shop is just five miles east of Disney's main gate, and through the routine of a pre-Disney Burger trip, she built a relationship with the close-knit club of locals who run all Burger operations: Patty has worked at Burger for a few years now, thanks to this Disney detour.

You could take the easy shot that this sort of analog fascination is a by-product of a digitally oversaturated age, and this particular wave of Burger fans—mostly young people who are the first generation to truly grow up with a digital life—is reacting against this, reviving classic formats to fulfill a lack of nostalgia for the album sleeve or the tape flip to give their cultural lives some texture. To focus on that aspect of Burger culture would be to neglect the dream, the building of another Magic Kingdom, because to buy into Burger is to buy into the hope that rock 'n' roll hasn't quite put out its last embers, that it can still keep us warm if we fan it.

"That magical shit … most people would chew it up, throw it out, and call it bullshit," Lee admits to me over the phone one evening. "But we're far out enough in our consciousness to get away with it." I ask him how he feels about Burger in this moment—its moment—and what has contributed to its rise. He muses on "eternal teenagers" as the most important ingredient of their thriving scene. It's the kind of kindred spirit that wouldn't mind stopping by the shop to pick up a Burger tape on the way to meet Mickey in Anaheim.

It was almost time for the nightly fireworks at Disneyland to explode above Anaheim, as they have for 60 years. If Burger stopped the movie they had on in the back room to listen, they'd be able to hear the glittering pops of the show, those exploding sparks of bursting light that drift into the smoggy softness of their nights. But they don't need to, because they know the story. They have lived it every night of their lives in Orange County, and are creating their own show, their own spectacle, their own narrative, their own sparks. They are building Burgerland. ✐

Dylan Tupper Rupert is an interdisciplinary designer and nonfiction writer. She is an original staff member of Rookie *and currently lives up and down the West Coast.*

Hold on Magnolia

The Tumultuous Rise and Fall of Jason Molina

BY ERIN OSMON

ILLUSTRATIONS BY JESS ROTTER

July 1, 2002, 10 days after the longest period of light that summer, Jason Molina stepped into the Chicago recording studio Electrical Audio for his own solstice. As the outside air sweltered 96 degrees over each of the session's three days, inside, the mind behind Songs: Ohia was a hot ball of energy. What resulted from that gathering of Molina's friends and musical collaborators, with engineer Steve Albini at the controls, is what many consider Molina's peak, *The Magnolia Electric Co.*, the sweetest fruits of the American songwriter's labor. The poor kid from Lorain, Ohio, soaring far beyond his five foot six frame—as high as that burning sun a week and a half ago. But the assembling of that studio cast, and the distinct shift in Molina's song craft, were many years in the making.

Drummer Jeff Panall was Molina's roommate at Oberlin College from 1993 to 1994, where Molina studied studio art and art history on a scholarship. They lived in a standard ramshackle college flop. There were nine guys total—some living between partitioned spaces in the living and dining rooms where bands would practice and play parties, and the young Molina would set up shop in the corner, often solo on ukulele, to perform for anyone who would listen. He played, invited or not, at the house parties that were the staple of campus social life at Oberlin, sometimes alone, sometimes with a drummer in tow. He quickly became a quirky fixture on the Oberlin scene, known to everyone as Sparky, a hated nickname earned for his unrelenting energy.

The first time Songs: Ohia bass player Rob Sullivan met Molina at Oberlin, the young misfit songwriter explained that he had just overheard a member of the city council at the grocery store saying Sullivan was going to be evicted from his apartment by the city. "I thought to myself, 'Hmmm. Is that really true, Sparky?'" Sullivan recalled. It wasn't. And neither were many of the stories Molina told, tall tales that became synonymous with the singer-songwriter, and something everyone in his life simply accepted about him.

Many theories exist about Molina's penchant for tall-tale telling, but the most concrete one comes from his younger brother Aaron, who attributes the trait to their father, a public school teacher in Lorain. "My dad is a big-time storyteller, and Jason totally got that from him," the younger Molina explained with some hesitation, before adding that he'd rather not dive too deeply into it.

"I don't think I realized it at first," Darcie Molina said of her late husband's tendency toward half-truths. "Why would you assume that the person you love and are married to is lying? If he were telling a story, I would believe him. There were certainly phases because we were together for 15 years. It wasn't an issue at all in the beginning, and then I noticed the exaggerations, and toward the end I just didn't believe anything he would say."

One of the most beloved Molina tall tales involved a photograph from his high school prom that Panall and another roommate, Tom Colley, found in a box of junk in the flophouse living room. "He was in a tux and his hair was all done up," Panall recalled. "So of course we put it up on the wall." When Molina returned home and his roommates razzed him about the pubescent relic, Molina responded soberly that it was difficult for him to look at it because the girl in the photograph had died in a terrible car wreck some time after that night. Though they left the photo on the wall, Panall and Colley eased up on the teasing—that is, until the girl from the photograph showed up on their front porch. "Our housemate was home one day, and someone knocked on the door. It was the woman from the picture," Colley said, before bursting into laughter. The woman still lived in Lorain, a 30-minute drive to Oberlin, and had decided to pop in to see how Molina was doing. When confronted about the lie, Colley said Molina pleaded ignorance, something to the effect, "Oh, really? Did I say that?"

Molina told many stories in his life, some with enough truth or purported facts to seem believable. "There's a guy named Molina in the band Crazy Horse [drummer Ralph Molina] that Sparky would say is his uncle or some sort of relative," Colley said. "I don't know if that's true or not. I never figured it out." Rob Sullivan remembers another story in which Molina insisted that his dad was, or could have been, a professional baseball player. Molina also told Colley and a few others that his brother worked for the CIA. However, sometimes the tales that seemed like the biggest whoppers turned out to be true, like the story of Glen Hansard. Panall and Dan Sullivan, Rob Sullivan's younger brother who played guitar in the band after Molina moved to Chicago, both remember Molina very casually mentioning that some sort of Irish celebrity was a

Molina responded soberly that it was difficult for him to look at it because the girl in the photograph had died in a terrible car wreck some time after that night. Though they left the photo on the wall, Panall and Colley eased up on the teasing—that is, until the girl from the photograph showed up on their front porch.

big fan and wanted to fly them to Dublin for a weekend to play some shows. A few weeks later Sullivan, Panall, and Molina boarded a plane.

⧓

Colley, who wasn't a musician but would make the Oberlin-to-Chicago trek, as many of Molina's Songs: Ohia comrades did, recorded some of Molina's early songs at WOBC FM, the campus radio station. Those youthful tapes, recorded in 1994 and 1995, reveal a charming inexperience, but the formula was there, and with more time spent soaking in life's earthy char, Molina would open up and pour out something complex and utterly enchanting that would mark his name in the minds of connoisseurs everywhere.

The Black Album—the first Songs: Ohia LP—poured out a couple of years later, and was released in the spring of 1997. But before that, there was a 7-inch, "Nor Cease Thou Never Now," released in 1996 on Will Oldham's Drag City-distributed Palace imprint. Colley and Panall were big fans of the mysterious Palace Brothers, and had planned to drive to Cleveland to catch Oldham's early band live for the first time. "Sparky couldn't go because he was too young," Colley recalled. "I'm fairly certain that Sparky didn't know their music that much, but we had said to him, 'Yeah, this is kind of like you.'" Molina placed a demo in Colley's trust with strict instructions to hand it to Oldham. "I can't remember if it was his idea or if someone else told him to do it," Colley added. "But I remember I was somewhat embarrassed and shy at the end of the show when I was like, 'Here's my friend's cassette, you should listen to it.'" Sometime thereafter Oldham contacted Molina to do the single, which eventually made its way into the ears of the young Swanson brothers, Chris and Ben, who had just formed their Secretly Canadian label in Bloomington, Indiana.

"**H**e was this little weird guy with a teenage mustache. He'd set up in the corner at parties with his ukulele, totally uninvited," said bassist Dan MacAdam. "He'd take your things, and they'd somehow become his. But it's almost impossible to get mad at him, even when he would do something that by normal standards would be shitty. The way he went about it seemed so not malicious, and he had his own way that he understood it in his head."

A couple of years before their younger friend graduated from Oberlin, MacAdam, Panall, and Colley packed up for Chicago and formed the Butcher Shop collective in an industrial warehouse space on Lake Street on the west side of Chicago. The space became an important DIY hub for the fringe art and music scenes that hosted epic parties and where the three friends operated a screen-printing shop. "As we were working here, we became the flophouse for all of our friends who were playing in bands like Trans Am, Oneida, and Golden, who'd stay on the floor while on tour," MacAdam explained. "Sparky came through with early Songs: Ohia before he moved here."

MacAdam still works in the space, which is now called Crosshair, where he continues to design and screen print posters for a range of bands and corporate clients. Walking across the second-floor loft's creaky boards, covered in varying dust and debris, he reached onto a shelf and pulled out a stack of sleeves for Molina's first 7-inch on Secretly Canadian, "One Pronunciation of Glory," which were designed and pressed by the hands of Panall, Colley, and MacAdam in 1996. The unfolded jackets appear lovingly handmade, with slight imperfections in the ink across the thick card stock. "We printed his early T-shirts and *The Black*

Contrary to his music, Molina was quite silly in life and always the first to crack a joke.

Album, too, which I've got here." Again, a stack of history any Molina fan would kill to have. "This is one of the first things we printed on this press," he said, as he pointed to a large and rather unwieldy looking iron machine. "It was very much the DIY dream/nightmare where none of us were technical or businessmen and we were trying to do something technical as a business." Across the street sits the Peoria Lunch Box, the take-out counter that inspired *Magnolia*'s second track on side two: "Peoria Lunch Box Blues."

The Butcher Shop was also famous for its annual holiday party, which required guests to wear seasonal garb as the collective's Christmas band, Dave LaCrone and the Mistletones, played covers of classic holiday tunes. The Sullivan brothers, who had relocated to Chicago, too, recruited an organ player, a friend of a friend who lived and worked in Hyde Park. "The first time I met Sparky was at a Mistletones practice," Jim

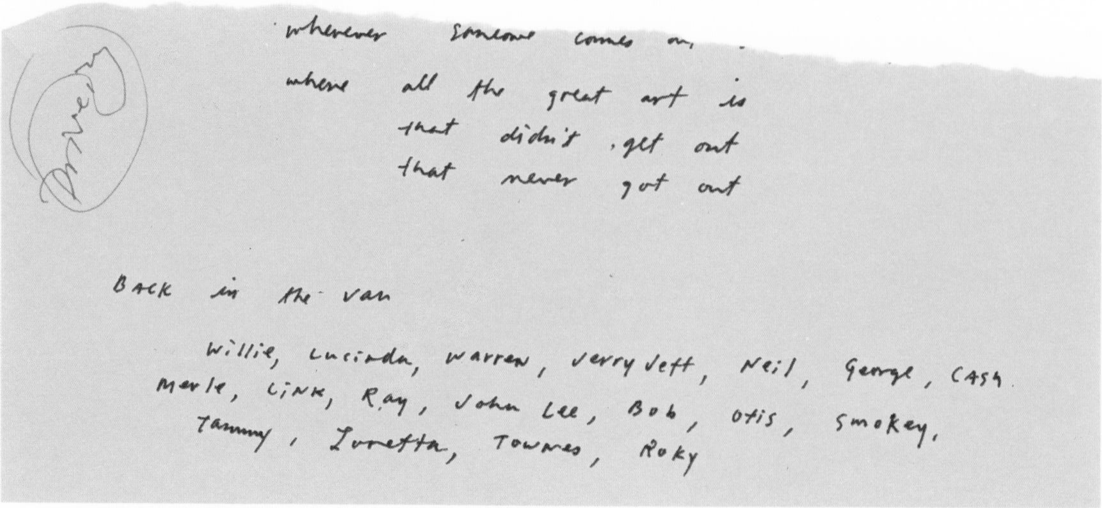

wherever someone comes on,
where all the great art is
that didn't get out
that never got out

Back in the van

Willie, Lucinda, warren, Jerry Jeff, Neil, George, Cash,
Merle, Link, Ray, John Lee, Bob, Otis, Smokey,
Tammy, Loretta, Townes, Roky

Molina wrote constantly, and often gave lyrics and poems as gifts to friends and fans.

Grabowski remembered. "He had volunteered to sing 'All I Want for Christmas is My Two Front Teeth.'" With a full-time job as a therapist, Grabowski didn't have the flexibility for the touring life, but learned the songs and helped out on piano and organ at local shows when he could.

By the turn of the century, the Chicago core of Songs: Ohia consisted of Panall on drums, Dan Sullivan on guitar, MacAdam on bass, and Grabowski on keys, with Rob Sullivan filling in on bass occasionally as well. "When I was in the band, Dan Sullivan was sort of the music director," Grabowski explained. "Sparky would show us the songs and Dan, with Sparky's permission, would show us what to play. Like ways to add texture and complexity without bumping into each other because the songs were so simple."

But contrary to his lyrical instructions on *Magnolia's* third track, "Just Be Simple," and to the nature of his two- or three-chord songs, working with Molina was anything but a cinch. "Molina is a very binary person," Secretly Canadian co-founder Chris Swanson said. "He's either immediately embracing what you're saying, or he's immediately rejecting you. There were ecstatic truths with him and you couldn't get caught trying too hard to strategize. He'd immediately shut it down." In the Songs: Ohia-era, Molina insisted upon the project as being his alone, regardless of how much freedom for interpretation or arrangement he gave his

players. Songs: Ohia was Molina, and no one else. He maintained that authority by a constant shuffling of personnel, yet the Oberlin-via-Chicago cast held tenure (mostly for touring) the longest.

Molina had a commitment to artistic authenticity, which manifested itself in the form of very little rehearsal, changing things up at the last minute, and absolutely no overdubs in the studio. He'd set up intricate patterns of musical dominoes, only to nonchalantly tip one over to see how many would fall. It was his way of instilling trust into his musicians, allowing their natural ability and reactions to his booby traps help tell his song's story. The fact that the Chicago-based core of Songs: Ohia was never invited into the studio only reinforced Molina's love of the slightly unhinged. Instead, he'd assemble a cast of musician friends and acquaintances, cherry-picked for reasons known only to him, and leave town to record the two albums he made during this phase of the band, *Ghost Tropic* and *Didn't It Rain*. "When he went and recorded *Didn't It Rain*, some of us had been playing with him for years," Panall said. "And we had been playing a completely different set of material. I think the drummer and the bass player on *Didn't It Rain* had never played with him before, and they probably only did one or two takes, and probably never played with him again."

That all changed with *Magnolia Electric Co.* A cast of friends, mostly from or related to the Oberlin scene,

Molina was never business minded—it was always about the craft—

which aligned with his Luddite tendencies and fascination with

maintaining the persona of a salt-of-the-earth workingman.

were invited into the studio to perform a new set of songs that were actually more like traditional rock music, with multiple chords and parts. Grabowski recalled Molina explaining that he had written new songs that were more like country songs or songs that you'd hear on the radio. And finally, after years of playing together, Songs: Ohia alumni Panall, Rob and Dan Sullivan, MacAdam, and Grabowski met at 2621 W. Belmont Avenue for what many describe as lightning in a bottle, a mystical conjuring of sonic spirits in Electrical Audio's Studio B. The *Magnolia Electric Co.* sessions also included guest vocalists Jennie Benford, a bluegrass musician from Molina's Oberlin days who appeared on *Didn't It Rain*; Lawrence Peters, a Chicago country singer and friend of Molina; Scout Niblett, a Secretly Canadian recording artist who Molina discovered while on tour in the UK; and lap steel player Mike Brenner from the *Didn't It Rain* session.

Peters recalled that, during the sessions, Molina had the posture of an Olympic athlete, "as if his whole life's work was coming down to this one moment." Others remembered him buzzing around the studio at a hummingbird's pace, intent on getting every song in one or two takes, observing and playing with a watchful eye, while massaging the songs with last-minute shuffling. "I showed up expecting to play a couple of violin parts and then leave," MacAdam remembered. "But Jason was like, 'We're recording a song. Go step up to the mic with Lawrence and sing.'" The song was "Farewell Transmission" and that's MacAdam and Peters cooing the line "long dark blues." The biggest surprise was when Molina asked MacAdam to handle guitar duties. "We were recording 'John Henry Split My Heart,' and I was playing violin and Jason said, 'Hey Dan, why don't you play guitar?'" What MacAdam didn't know was that Sullivan had not shown up for the third day of the session. "I was blissfully unaware of what was going on. I didn't have a part, but I went to the basement where Steve Albini's guitars are, and I was like, 'I'm going to play the Rapeman guitar!' The same thing happened with 'Almost Was Good Enough.'"

"I didn't really know this drama thing was going on,"

Brenner adds. A few palpably strained moments between Molina and Dan Sullivan aside, no one else really did, either. Sullivan said it started a couple of weeks before the session at Electrical, when he received the demos. "Molina was casually like, 'Here's the record we're making,'" Dan Sullivan explained. "I became frustrated because it was so far from what I had become comfortable playing with him, and at that point I sort of knew that he and I were done." What happened next would contribute to a shift not just in studio personnel, but Molina's entire outlook on Songs: Ohia.

"What I really didn't want to do was fuck up the session," Sullivan said. "We all knew we were making a great album. There was this big cast of characters and everyone was bringing their best, myself included, even though I was frustrated. There had been some intense moments of me feeling humiliated because my input had been shot down, whereas before I had had such an open dialogue with him. And it was his right! It was his record, and it turned out beautifully. I tried my best to just be a bit player, and do what I was told. But I was pissed off and feeling like a hypocrite, so I played the first two days and then left." Some players thought Molina had instituted one of his famous firings. The band had dubbed these displays, which rarely stuck, "Songs: I'll Fire Ya."

Dan Sullivan said his departure from the *Magnolia* session was voluntary. "I actually showed up the morning of the third day, but he wasn't there. I was ready to talk to him about it, about how I wasn't happy," Sullivan recalled. "He called me later and chewed me out. I was wrecked because my brother and all my friends were there, and we had made this great thing. But my experience making this record was terrible. It just took a time to get over that. It was obviously the end. I loved it so much, and when I couldn't be a part of it any more, it just broke my heart."

His departure wasn't even the biggest shake-up that Songs: Ohia experienced during that session. It was then, too, that Molina announced, casually, that he had decided to move to Bloomington. "I didn't appreciate how shocking it was because I wasn't really there for these other

Some players thought Molina had instituted one of his famous firings.

The band had dubbed these displays, which rarely stuck, "Songs: I'll Fire Ya."

bombs that he would drop," Grabowski said. "I thought, 'that's too bad,' and assumed these other guys had heard about it before because of the way he had said it."

Ben Swanson said Molina returned to Bloomington with the two-inch tapes from the *Magnolia* session labeled NOT SONGS: OHIA, and that he was dying to start a more traditional band with consistent players. "I don't think it was only because of the Sullivan experience, but it was informative," Swanson explained, and added that Jason and Dan could both be fiery, which is the reason they had chemistry, but also the reason they infuriated one another. "I think Jason had this idea of the recording process in his brain and Dan encroached on that, and probably went a little too far and Jason over-reacted a little too much," he added. "Part of it, too, was that Jason knew he had created a really unique record, different from what he had done in the past, and he saw the power of a truly great band."

Molina had actually threatened to change the Songs: Ohia name ever since he began making records under that peculiar moniker, and he reveled in a certain level of anxiety among his collaborators, Secretly Canadian included. Rob Sullivan remembered Molina telling him that he planned to change the name of the band after the release of *Magnolia Electric Co*. "He was kind of opaque about it, and I didn't really believe him, until he did it," he said. "But that was like many Jason Molina things." Molina was never business minded—it was always about the craft—which aligned with his Luddite tendencies and fascination with maintaining the persona of a salt-of-the-earth workingman. He believed that, as long as he continued to construct exceptional records, he would be successful.

Some say Secretly Canadian released *Magnolia* under the Songs: Ohia band name for marketing purposes and to sell records, but according to Chris Swanson, Molina didn't yet have a new name for the band. "He probably had the idea for a band named Magnolia Electric Co., and then he decided to name the record that," he said. "And sometimes he'd say that it was the first Magnolia Electric Co. record, but that's an act of convenience. He was being whimsical with the truth there." It wasn't until Molina made the distinction

that he wanted to start a band, rather than soldier on a lone wolf with a rotating cast of characters under a new name, that the label got on board. "We were very excited and very proud that he chose a Bloomington band," Swanson added. "We were proud that he chose to live in Bloomington. It legitimized something about our relationship."

Magnolia Electric Co. was released in April 2003, to critical acclaim. It remains Molina's best-selling album to date. For the first time Molina had rounded up a group of permanent collaborators, a rock band under the banner of that album's namesake, consisting of Bloomington-based musicians Pete Schreiner (drums and bass), Jason Groth (guitar), Michael Kapinus (bass and piano) and Mark Rice (drums), friends who had played in the The Coke Dares, a raucous garage-punk act whose raw energy had impressed Molina. "The Coke Dares were perfect for Molina because they were totally unpretentious," Chris Swanson said. Molina recruited Groth, Schreiner, and Kapinus in 2002, shortly after he moved to Bloomington, and the quartet toured on the *Magnolia* album and recorded material while still under the Songs: Ohia name. "Molina always told us that the guys from the *Magnolia* record couldn't tour, so we didn't think there were any hard feelings," Schreiner said. "Maybe those guys felt differently at the time, but we had no idea." The new Songs: Ohia learned of the name change from a post on *Pitchfork*, not from the mouth of Molina himself.

Jason Groth initially noticed Molina's excessive and secretive drinking in 2005. "I think he had been kind of a teetotaler before that," he added, noting that he had heard stories that Molina very rarely drank during his Songs: Ohia years. However, about three years after the name switch, he began drinking much more heavily. "One minute he'd be normal, and then he'd go away for, what seemed like five minutes, and come back totally smashed," Groth remembered. "He would say things like he was on medication, but that never turned out to be true." It often interfered with Molina's ability to perform and, at its most extreme, the rest of the band would instruct the sound guys at the clubs where Magnolia Electric Co. played to turn Molina's guitar all the way down and out of the mix. "Some musicians can get drunk and play just fine," said Groth. "But he wasn't like that at all. His voice would suffer and his guitar playing would suffer tremendously."

What the band didn't fully realize at the time was that Molina couldn't control his secretive binge drinking. "The shape of that curve was definitely a trumpet," Schreiner explained. "It grew over time." At first the four bandmates thought Molina might have been purposefully sabotaging shows as a reaction to the band gaining more exposure. Press coverage had picked up drastically since the release of *Magnolia* the album, and had carried through to 2005's *What Comes After the Blues* and that same year's live album *Trials & Errors*, the first two releases under the Magnolia Electric name. After the prolificacy of his Songs: Ohia period, Molina's once furious writing paced slowed to a near halt: between 2005 and 2008, the quintet played almost the same set, consisting of material they had been playing for as long as two years before. Molina's songwriting drought and binge drinking were a chicken-and-egg scenario, though, in that no one knew which one came first—whether Molina was suffering writer's block and began drinking as a means to self medicate, or whether his drinking was the product of some other demon and caused his pace to slow as he became addicted.

"He just seemed to be getting weirder," Dan Sullivan said of Molina's Magnolia years. At that point the two former musical collaborators saw each other only once or twice a year, usually when Molina and his new band of brothers would roll through town. But his idiosyncrasies seemed to be escalating. "He could always talk a lot, and he never really asked you about yourself, but that wall seemed to be getting bigger," Sullivan continued. That manic energy existed when the two had played together, too. But at that time it was a good thing, Sullivan insisted. "It contributed to the strength of the music, which had some pretty dark stuff. But that was not a conversation you were going to have with him."

"What used to be fun and silly about Sparky's tall tales—whether his brother was in the CIA, or that girl died, or his uncle was in Crazy Horse—it didn't matter. He was an amazing storyteller and that's one of the things I loved about him," Colley said. "But when things got really bad with his drinking, he started telling lies and stories about things that did matter and that was really hard."

Groth's assessment aligns with Sullivan's. "He talked forever and deciphering what he meant became increasingly difficult. The stories would change. The reasons for drinking would change." It got to the point where the band instituted "sober tours" in which none of the band members would drink, "in order to cultivate a culture of sobriety," Groth said. At times it felt to the band like they were managing a child. It had gotten to the point where Molina complained about everything and what he did enjoy or approve of was mind boggling, like ordering chicken fingers at a three-star restaurant. He became temperamental, increasingly critical of audiences and, in the words of Groth, "kind of bratty," refusing to do encores or interact with audiences at all. On the band's last tour, in support of 2009's *Josephine*, Groth kept a tour diary of the details, as he and the rest of the band knew it would be the last go.

10/19/09

Sevilla, Spain

We discovered a square that had a restaurant with cheap tapas and lots of outdoor seating. The octopus and potato salad and the risotto were unbelievably good, but what wasn't good was drunken Molina. He made it through two very tall glasses of red wine on top of whatever else he was drinking during the day, and was talking and talking and interrupting and touching food that he had no intention of eating. He was in full-on drunkarexic mode (i.e., the buzz was obviously pretty good, and food would do nothing but shut it down and put him to sleep). On the way back we stopped at a gelato place and Molina was swerving all over the street. I told him to watch Mikey and concentrate. My biggest concern was him falling into the cobblestone street right in the path of a car or scooter. There were a few close calls. Finally we arrived at the hotel and made sure that our inebriated brother got into his room.

> "It's almost impossible to get mad at him, even when he would do something that by normal standards would be shitty. The way he went about it seemed so not malicious, and he had his own way that he understood it in his head." —DAN MacADAM

Shortly after the tour, Darcie Molina and the band would finally connect, after concerted efforts by the ailing Molina to keep them apart. "He knew if we compared stories, he would be in trouble," she said. After exchanging notes, Darcie was finally able to convince her very resistant and denial-riddled husband into his first rehabilitation program outside of London, where the couple had been living since 2007.

After rehabilitation attempts in London failed, Darcie realized she could no longer handle Molina on her own, and it was decided by his friends and family that he would do better stateside, in a familiar community of supporters. The Chicago-based former members of Songs: Ohia banded together to get their ailing friend into rehab in the city he once loved so much. When that didn't take, Molina's Bloomington band hatched a similar plan for a program in Indianapolis. And after two separate trials there, an escape to New Orleans, and stints in programs with the support of his family in West Virginia, Molina succumbed on March 16, 2013, at age 39.

From one perspective, it isn't terribly dramatic, as he died the almost textbook death of an alcoholic. It seemed the only time Molina acknowledged his demon was before it had parasitically attached itself to its host. "In Chicago, he and I would talk about the fact that he's probably an alcoholic, from a physical or medical sense, before it was an actual problem," Darcie Molina explained. "Like the fact that it runs in the family, and if he were to start drinking heavily he would be physically and mentally addicted to alcohol. Almost like an inactive disease."

After his passing, a memorial and series of tribute shows were organized in 2014, as a way for both his Songs: Ohia and Magnolia bandmates to celebrate their fallen comrade. Secretly Canadian reissued Molina's magnum opus in November 2013, in honor of its 10th anniversary, and it included Sullivan's version of the previously unissued "The Big Game Is Every Night," a track the guitarist said really clicked between he and Molina. "And the last thing I see / Let it be me helping honestly / Let it be me working / On being a better me," Molina quivers over Sullivan's guitar, which makes smooth, elegant cuts through the thick atmosphere, carving slivers for Molina's guts to spill out all over the place. Much to the dismay of so many who loved the idiosyncratic songwriter, the work outside the work proved not enough.

But he left so many gifts along the way, including that prodigious album captured over those three days in July. As he sang in *Magnolia Electric Co.*'s signature track, the very prescient "Farewell Transmission": "I will be gone / But not forever." ✐

Erin Osmon is a Chicago-based writer. Her work has appeared in Chicago Magazine, Chicago Reader, Chicago Tribune, Chicago Sun-Times, Time Out Chicago *and* The A.V. Club. *Her fascination with Jason Molina began in high school in 1997, when she discovered* The Black Album *after hitching a ride to Kentucky to buy records at Ear X-Tacy. For the last year she has been researching and writing* Riding with the Ghost, *her forthcoming book on Molina.*

CIRCULATION DESK

Subjects include Korean Starbucks, Imprisoned Pussy, and Punk Puke

BOOK REVIEWS
by J.R. Nelson

Let any true believer run rampant for 160 pages about an album that obsesses them and they're bound to sink into some me-first morass. Some titles in Bloomsbury's 33 1/3 series—book-length considerations of classic albums coddled by critics, musicians, and academics—are often at their most instructive and appealing in that very mode: Matmos' Drew Daniel becoming immersed in Throbbing Gristle's music and sneaking into the "death factory" of a rendering plant leads to unsettling and prescient observations. But just as often these little books disappear deep into the dregs. We're minus one shady grove of trees so The Decemberists' front man Colin Meloy could paper over The Replacement's *Let It Be* with an unbearably precious take on his childhood.

Veteran rock writer Gina Arnold spends much of her entry on Liz Phair's 1993 indie-rock masterpiece *Exile in Guyville* zigging and zagging between autobiographical nattering and salient criticism. Should we be expected to care about the South Korean Starbucks where she writes and gets her free Wi-Fi, and subsequent mini-essay on how the chain went from neighborhood coffeehouse to worldwide corporate behemoth? Not so much. Her scrutiny of the original mid-'90s reaction to *Exile* is thorough—spotlighting the blatant sexism that cropped up in comments from local Chicago critics and fanzine scribes insisting her sound was manufactured by producer Brad Wood, and the leering fixation of the national music press on Phair's employment of "dirty words," and their affront by her sexual candor. As she rightly notes, "sex in the mouth of a woman is generally willfully interpreted (by men) to be an erotic call for action," and that despite topping many critics' lists, reactions to the record were almost uniformly reflected through the male gaze.

In a meandering middle section, where Arnold begins to compare Phair's album to the The Rolling Stones' *Exile on Main Street*, the LP it famously responds to, Arnold seems exasperated that Phair didn't become a bigger commercial force, yet she's dismissive of cultural ubiquity, riffing on the Stones' "earning potential" and "life of a band" in a confusing quasi-Nietzschean framework. She biffs on obvious topics, too—*Cocksucker Blues* being sexist garbage isn't exactly a news flash. Her arguments about inequality in San Francisco, Jay-Z and Rihanna, and the superstar system's "field of musical production," are enough to make any reader give up.

I'm glad I didn't. Arnold's truncated track-to-track comparison of the two albums contains the book's most incisive work. She is especially strong on *Guyville*'s last two songs, "Stratford-on-Guy" and "Strange Loop." Arnold abandons her *Exile* vs. *Exile* template and draws comparison between "Stratford" and the opening scene of Dreiser's *Sister Carrie*—and it's elucidating and engaging work.

What truly discourages is that Arnold gives the ghosts of *Guyville* far more say than Phair's music. Apart from a paragraph-long email from Matador Records honcho Gerard Cosloy, none of the major players—including Phair herself—are interviewed. Arnold's conclusion that "the record doesn't really need that backstory to stand on its own musical merits. The narrative and

emotional appeals it makes are strong enough to stand the test of time" seems to have the effect of invalidating most of her own book. Regardless, Phair's album came to prevail and be regarded as a masterpiece because listeners came to recognize her life in exile—all those bad roommates, shit-talking scenesters, and distant yet predatory dudes—and see it as their own. I wish we'd heard more about it from the source.

Instead of suffering a cloistered music scene, this decade's most strident, fearless punks are in a stupefyingly brave all-out war with state power. When three members of Russian feminist punk collective Pussy Riot — Nadya Tolokonnikova, Masha Alyokhina, and Katya Samutsevich—were convicted and sentenced to prison in 2012 for the dubious charge of "hooliganism and religious hatred" after performing a song called "Our Lady, Chase Putin Out" on the altar of a Moscow church, and the abject political corruption and sexism at work against them in their homeland began to peel back in layers, the surrealism of it all kept endlessly multiplying. A couple of years later, after they'd been freed from prison by Putin's brutal oligarchy and immediately protested against it again during the Sochi Winter Olympics—in the brightly colored tights, dresses, and balaclavas that remain their visual trademark—these women were attacked by drably uniform pro-government Cossacks with whips. To many Westerners, myself included, Pussy Riot's evolving story seems like a fractured fairy tale. (In six months, I half expect to read that Russian authorities have baked Pussy Riot into a pie.) When Amer-

ican punk bands enter courtrooms, they're usually fighting each other over a copyright.

In dry, fact-packed prose, Masha Gessen, a Russian-American best known for her dissident reporting on Putin and his regime, brings an intense rigor and unflinching eye to the labyrinthine tale of Pussy Riot's feminist and artistic development, trial, and imprisonment. *Words Will Break Cement* is easily the most complete one-stop data point on the story so far. While the Western media has done little more than ratchet up the obviousness of their own incomprehension—consider Brian Williams asking David Remnick on the *NBC Nightly News* if "Pussy Riot is onto something" and *60 Minutes'* Lesley Stahl referring to them as "lewd and crude" and making faces just saying their name out loud—Gessen was visiting Tolokonnikova in prison and conducting interviews with family members and cohorts. In spots, *Words Will Break Cement* reads as a manifesto and eloquent call to action: "In all societies, public rhetoric involves some measure of lying, and history—political history and art history—is made when someone effectively confronts the lie … they wanted to confront the language of lies that had been … reconstructed and reinforced, discrediting the language of confrontation itself. There were no words left."

Gessen's book reaches its peak during the 2012 "religious hate" trial, when the full farce of legal doublespeak is at its apogee. The only people who make any sense during the proceedings are Pussy Riot themselves. The prosecution, the judge, witnesses from the church testifying against them, and even the trio's defense attorneys, seem to be lost in false motives and Orwellian doublespeak. Gessen includes the women's major speeches from the courtroom in their own defense—some of the most essential, eloquent punk manifestos ever written, and under incredible duress, by the way. She is equally gutted when they are convicted and sentenced to two years in prison. Later portions of the book, where she reports on Tolokonnikova and Alyokhina (Samutsevich was released after seven months) performing hard labor in gulags, appealing against the brutal conditions of the prison system, and struggling to live apart from their children, makes for harrowing reading.

Tolokonnikova and Alyokhina's first major project after being released in December 2013 was to found Zona Prava, an advocacy organization for the rights of prisoners. The youth and energy of their activism only seems to have gotten started, and this is heartening because since their incarceration the majority of musically and intellectually forward-thinking rock music has been dominated by punk-as-fuck feminists. White Lung, Priests, Perfect Pussy, Downtown Boys, and Good Throb readily spring to mind. The powerful voices of these bands, along with Pussy Riot, remind us that we needn't always feed off the past's musty oxygen. We are free to receive their sounds through new air.

Execute Your Idols

OPENING FIRE WITH THE QUIP "BOB DYLAN BROKE HIS NECK—close, but no cigar" and ending with a love letter to Joan Jett and Poly Styrene, Julie Burchill and Tony Parson's *"The Boy Looked At Johnny." The Obituary of Rock and Roll* is a little shorter than a typical 33 1/3 book and as flimsy with its logic as a sheet of toilet paper. No matter. Dropped out of print and largely forgotten since it was published in the UK in 1978, it's also one of the most scabrous, hilarious "execute the scene," chopping-block polemics ever committed to type. Punks hired by the UK's *New Musical Express* weekly music rag in 1977 to make sense of the exploding Sex Pistols-led scene—at the ripe ages of 17 and 22, respectively—Burchill and Parsons instead took a blowtorch to every band in their path, cracking one-liners about sacred cows like The Jam ("a time warped souvenir sure to win favor within the reactionary mass ... Paul Weller is the Barry McGuire of punk"), The Damned ("tame and mercenary mindlessness"), and dozens of other unfortunates, dispensing questionable pharmaceutical advice ("amphetamine ... the only drug that makes you sit up and ask questions rather than lie down and lap up answers") along the way. Partisans of fanzine fury should cop this blistering treatise posthaste. ✐

I BELIEVE I'M GOING TO MAKE IT:

RE-EXAMINING THE SOULFUL SOUNDS OF JOE TEX

By Andy Beta

Illustrations by
Johnny Sampson

In 1969, Navasoto, Texas' proudest son, the soul singer Joe Tex, delivered a church-rooted ode to his grandmother. It begins like a sermon might, with the bold, soulful voice of Tex, accompanied by piano.

> CHILDREN COME AND
> GET THIS BREAD
> WHILE IT'S HOT.
> ONE OF Y'ALL FINISH THIS LIL'
> DAB OF MUSTARD GREENS
> SO I CAN WASH MY POT.
> YOU DON'T HAVE ENOUGH TO EAT,
> JUST FILL UP ON WATER.
> THANK THE LORD FOR
> THIS LITTLE BIT WE GOT.

The solemnity of the opening gives way to an endearing portrait of a young boy fondly remembering his grandmother. A skip-a-rope beat emerges, and the song matures into a hybrid of country and soul, guitar twang and bright horns commingling. Abject poverty surrounds the shoeless narrator, from the bellyful of water to his grandma asking her white employer for any discarded shoes. "I hope we get some shoes today," he says at one point. Grandma Mary has to buy meat on credit, so as to feed the family, though she has another request, too. "Don't forget yer grandma's snuff," which Joe Tex sings in lieu of a chorus.

In "Grandma Mary," Tex immortalizes Mary Richardson, the woman who raised him in rural Texas until the age of 12, with a subtle eye for detail akin to the sharpest short story writer. "People are my most important product," Tex once told a British journalist. Or, as he put it on another song, "You can find out anything you wanna know ... At Ida Mae's beauty shop / At Webb's barber shop / Or you can read it on the restroom wall / At the bus depot."

"Grandma Mary" is an album cut from the B-side of Joe Tex's most well-regarded album from the era,

1969's *Buying a Book*. It marked Tex's peak as a soul singer, cementing him as one of Atlantic Records' most notable acts on a roster overstuffed with soul icons: Solomon Burke, Aretha Franklin, Wilson Pickett, and the like. Author and soul aficionado Peter Guralnick mentions Tex in the same breath as virtuosic entertainers like Otis Redding and Jackie Wilson. And, unlike his contemporaries, Tex's tracks often crossed over to the pop charts. His stage show and fancy footwork were rivaled only by James Brown. But if Brown is considered the king of R&B, then Joe Tex is the court jester, throwing rocks at the throne (more on that later). He titled his 1972 album *From the Roots Came the Rapper*, and this proved prescient, as Tex laid the foundations for African-American music that lay just on the other side of funk and disco in the 1980s: hip-hop.

Yet try to buy an album like *Buying a Book* and you'll realize that it's out of print in the United States, available only via a dodgy import. (Thankfully, Spotify can be employed to fill in most of the blanks.) It's an ignoble end for one of southern soul's most peculiar acts, the rare soul singer who penned his own material. Tex did novelty as well as heartache, slick as well as gritty, a preacher as well as ribald jokester, detailing the nuances of small town morality when not grunting out sex jokes. Robert Christgau once wrote that Tex's "good-humored country wisdom rivaled Smokey [Robinson]'s urban variant for pith and empathy." Tex has been covered by country artists, rock bands—even Phish. But his singular talents as a songwriter don't readily transfer onto other singers. The breaks that Tex's salt-and-pepper backing band in Muscle Shoals and Nashville crafted didn't initially become the heartbeat of hip-hop like Brown's did. Outside of a few instances in hip-hop (name-checked by Madvillain, rapped over by J Dilla, sampled by The RZA on two early Wu-Tang tracks, echoed in the gruffness of a southern rapper like Mystikal) and inclusion by filmmaker Quentin Tarantino on the soundtracks to *Reservoir Dogs* and *Death Proof*, Joe Tex has all but vanished from the cultural landscape.

Joe Tex was born Joseph Arrington Jr., in Rogers, Texas, in 1935 and raised in neighboring Baytown. While still a junior in high school, he won a talent show, and then while in New York City, won amateur night at the Apollo four weeks in a row with his comedy routine, landing a contract with King Records (also home to James Brown). He returned to finish high school but was soon in the studio and touring the chitlin' circuit in

You know how James came out with the cape? Joe had one made up out of a raggedy blanket, with holes all in it. You know how James would break down and fall on his knees? Joe fell on his knees, and all of a sudden, he grabbed his back. He had the cape on and got all tangled up in it, and he was fighting to get out, singing, "Please, please, please, get me out of this cape." He just made a mockery of James.

At an after-hours club, James Brown exacted his revenge on Tex. Says Collier:

James took a couple of shotguns, and I think six people got shot. James did most of the shooting, and Joe was running back behind the trees and bushes. So that was the end of the Joe Tex / James Brown revue.

By the end of 1964, despite partnering with Nashville producer/lifelong friend Buddy Killen, Tex had no hits to show for a decade in the music business. Recording in a small studio run by Rick Hall in Muscle Shoals, Alabama, Tex and his band of funky white boys put down nearly seven hours of music for one single. But there was still some space left on the reel. With the upcoming holiday season, the band revamped the Christmas carol "Holy, Holy, Holy (Lord God Almighty)," while Tex, his singing voice ragged and hoarse from the session, rapped off the top of his head about his pregnant new wife, as well as the childhood sweetheart who had left him behind. Tex reportedly hated the song, begging Killen not to release it. But with a nimble splicing of different takes on the tape, "Hold What You've Got" was pressed and released without Tex's approval. By the time he learned about it a month later, some 200,000 copies had been shipped. The anguished yet redemptive ballad reached number one on the R&B charts and number five on the pop charts, the first of Tex's 30-plus hits.

the '50s. He had nearly a decade of non-hits, aping R&B stalwarts like Little Richard and quickly writing answer songs like "Pneumonia," which he wrote in response to Little Willie John's "Fever." (Tex reportedly wrote and sold it for $300 in a financial pinch.)

Problems with labelmate James Brown began when both Tex's first wife, Bea Ford, and one of Tex's songs, "Baby You're Right," wound up in Brown's hands, not to mention a now-famous stage trick that Tex had perfected in high school: kicking the microphone stand down and then popping it back up. The rivalry reached its boiling point in 1963 when Brown, flush from the success of his *Live at the Apollo* album, returned to his hometown of Macon, Georgia, to perform, with Joe Tex as the opener. As Newton Collier recounted in *Creative Loafing*'s 2007 James Brown oral history:

"Everybody was into the boogie-woogie, everybody was boogying and here came this cat with this slow ballad and it blew everybody's mind: Everybody in my neighborhood in Southeast Los Angeles thought it was the most refreshing new sound," Barry White remarked in a memorial episode of *Soul Train* soon after Tex's untimely passing. "Joe exploded on the horizon.

He wasn't just a singer: he was a songwriter, a producer, arranger, a musician. He was young, gifted, and black."

"Hold What You've Got" allowed Tex to buy his Grandma Mary a house, and it also opened up the floodgates for a series of inimitable, idiosyncratic soul singles. Looking at his mid-'60s chart-topping sides, there was the breakneck foodie rave-up of "Chicken Crazy"; the happy soul of "Show Me"; the southern colloquialisms of "One Monkey Don't Stop No Show" and "Heep See Few Know"; the heartbreaking ballad "The Love You Save"; a stand-up routine about the cankle-less on "Skinny Legs and All"; and the infectious but entangled chorus of "S.Y.S.L.J.F.M. (The Letter Song)." And that's before he later delved into hard funk about stinky feet, dancing with sissies, or—even harder—with heavyset women on his last chart hit, "Ain't Gonna Bump No More (With No Big Fat Woman)."

Preaching, grunting, and clowning in equal measure, appearing on *Soul Train* in hoedown lederhosen, Tex joked around in one raunchy, winking song, so as to be that much more disarming and directly honest in the next. Christgau noted in one review that Tex was "a novelty artist whose subject is morality," and in the first edition of his book on hip-hop, *Rap Attack*, David Toop traced the nascent genre's roots back to Tex: "His raps hovered on the edge of being stand-up comic routines. The same ambivalence can be found in many soul raps—in most instances they exist in the context of songs, drawing on preaching, comedy and soap-opera drama."

Tex was also the first pop star to address the Vietnam War, with 1966's "I Believe I'm Gonna Make It," and he cagily couched the message of civil rights amid the strut of "We Can't Sit Down Now." On his routines-as-songs, Tex connects the generation of chitlin' circuit comedians like Redd Foxx and Pigmeat Markham to the next generation of stand-ups like Richard Pryor (who himself used to sing the blues). Slow ballads like "Hold What You Got" and "The Love You Save (May Be Your Own)," as well as gentle odes like "Sweet, Sweet Woman" and "That's the Way," reveal a down-home moralism that makes me think of Sam the Lion in *The Last Picture Show*, the wise heart of a slowly expiring small Texas town.

Across his body of work, Tex tsk-tsks his head at gossip, at the notion of "buying a book," not to mention the vanity, foolishness, apathy, and racism that crop up in both men and women, on either side of the tracks, in small towns and large metropolises. Across an arc of songs like "Keep the One You Got," "Woman Stealer," "Hold What You Got," "The Same Things It Took to Get Me," Tex addresses that peculiar misconception of reality: that someone has it better than you, that the bird not in your hand but across the street was the one you wanted. "Don't she look good?" he sings of that woman over there, then posits the flip of such desire: "But she might not be as good as she looks." In Tex's moralistic universe, there was no greater sin than coveting thy neighbor's wife and not appreciating and respecting the love you already got. (A close second is the despised hometown hero in "You Need Me Baby" who calls it "a little one-horse town full of jive people" as he breaks out for the big city.)

Even in the midst of the civil rights movement, of witnessing the severe brutality of the South as a black man in the '60s, a lack of love was, for Joe Tex, the biggest inhumanity of them all. "The Love You Save (May Be Your Own)" (not to be confused with the Jackson 5 tune) remains one of the most brutal soul ballads of that or any other era, and Tex pulls no punches in detailing the savage treatment he received at the hands of others:

I'VE BEEN PUSHED AROUND, I'VE BEEN LOST AND FOUND. I'VE BEEN GIVEN 'TIL SUNDOWN TO GET OUT OF TOWN I'VE BEEN TAKEN OUTSIDE AND I'VE BEEN BRUTALIZED AND I HAD TO ALWAYS BE THE ONE TO SMILE AND APOLOGIZE.

Harrowing and awful as those admissions are, Tex sees beyond the politics and race and savagery to the underlying crime: "I ain't never in my life before / Seen so many love affairs go wrong as I do today." With a little more love, by taking the time to stop and find out what's wrong with your lover, he tells us, these other injustices could be overcome.

One of my favorite Joe Tex songs leads off the otherwise unremarkable 1968 album *Soul Country* (it includes a cover of "Ode to Billie Joe" that verges on the homoerotic when Billie Joe puts a bullfrog down his pants). "I'll Never Do You Wrong" appears on the surface to just be a little ditty about love, and even has insipid, simpleton rhyme schemes to match: fly/pie/eye, sore/elbow/toe. As the horns gently nudge toward a climax, the words give way to something deeper beneath the soulful pop surface. It's about love, sure, the promises of love, but a love that secretly acknowledges pain, and it comes to light that what happens to the lover also happens to the beloved.

Around 1968, Tex accepted the Muslim faith, renaming himself Joseph Hazziez and preaching as Minister Joseph X. Harrington. "There was a void in my spiritual life," he told British writer Cliff White. "The material thing: I had accomplished that. After 10 years I had a beautiful wife, my son, hit records ... and we were financially stable, but the spiritual part was missing. In 1966, I went into Muhammad's Temple in Miami and heard the minister teach and, hey man, it hit me like a ton of bricks."

By 1972, he focused on his newfound faith more than his recording career. Even with such faith to steady him through a decrease in performances and the changing tide of soul music into disco, Tex man-

aged to score intermittent hits. But as the decade came to a close, pressures from the IRS, other women, and hangers-on caught up with him. As Buddy Killen put it: "Joe Tex lived almost his entire life without alcohol or drugs. Then, during his last four years, he staged a marathon of self-abuse; it was as if he were trying to make up for lost time." In August of 1982, he was found at the bottom of his East Texas swimming pool, but he was soon resuscitated and sent home. Just a few days on, though, he suffered a heart attack and died in the hospital at the age of 47.

Had he lived, there's a chance Tex might have had renewed relevance for the "roots" generation, or at the very least been put in a studio and embalmed by producers like Rick Rubin or Joe Henry. For all of his proto-hip-hop credentials, the grit and wit of Tex didn't crop up too often in the throats of East Coast rappers, but when the south rose—with the likes of Master P, UGK, Mannie Fresh, and Three 6 Mafia—Tex's influence could be heard once again, raunchy, funny, dead-serious, and profound in equal measure.

"Why is it, when a black artist dies, it's business as usual?" host Don Cornelius rhetorically asks of Barry White on that commemorative episode of *Soul Train*. It's a serious question, and both men are visibly shaken at the loss. And yet, solemn as they are, when they mention Tex's last chart hit, "Ain't Gonna Bump No More (With No Big Fat Woman)," both men can't help it; they bust into laughter in unison. ✎

Andy Beta loves disco, techno, new age, reggae, rock, and more and writes about it all for The Wall Street Journal, SPIN, Rolling Stone, NPR, Wondering Sound, *and* Pitchfork.

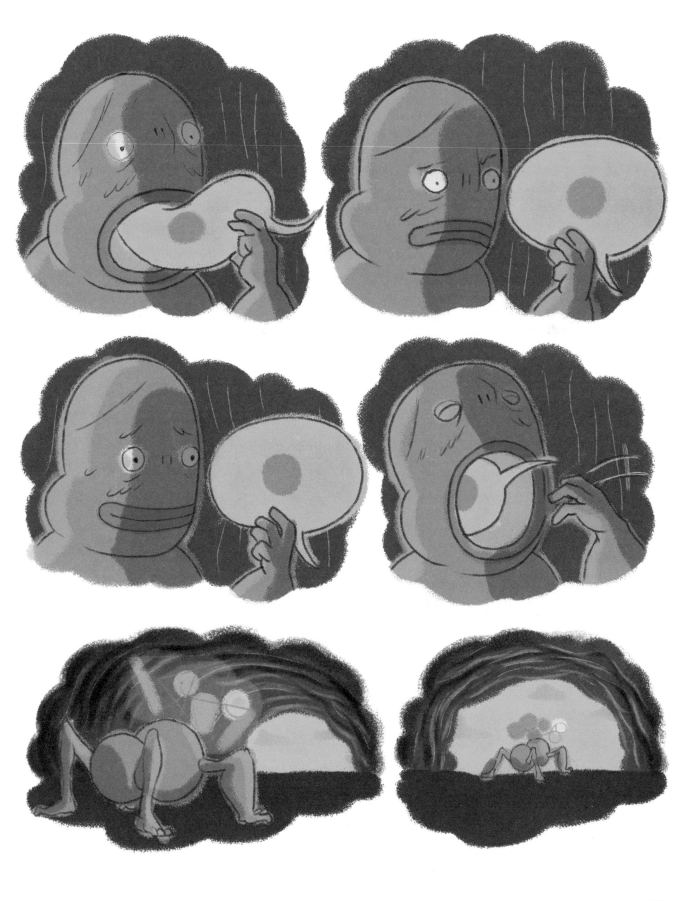

Male Movement and Sex Machines in Contemporary Black Music

Pop, dat Dick Up

by Joshua Alston

It holds true that the more irresistible a narrative is, the greater the odds it veers closer to apocrypha than fact. The unraveling of D'Angelo, and the artistic drought that came in its wake, is one such story. The story may not be objectively true, but it's much like D'Angelo himself in the music video often cited for cracking his mirror and derailing his auspicious career. The story of D'Angelo's decline is seductive, unusual, and instructive in any conversation about how black men express themselves physically through music.

The conventional wisdom on why D'Angelo hasn't released a new studio recording in 14 years has its roots in a *SPIN* feature from August 2008. Stark and unflattering, its title—"D'Angelo: What the Hell Happened?"—seemed the only suitable header. At that time, the public's image of D'Angelo wasn't his star-making turn in the video for "Untitled (How Does It Feel)," in which he appeared nude, forged from chocolate diamonds, and displayed as if on a rotating cake stand. As indelible as that image was, it couldn't compare with his then-recent mug shot, in which he appeared 40 pounds heavier without a cell of muscle, and with his face trapped in the 1,000-yard stare typical of men arrested for soliciting a prostitute. The *SPIN* piece drew a straight, bright line between the former D'Angelo and the latter. The theory was simple: turning into an overnight sex symbol shattered D'Angelo's psyche and made him feel insecure about his music. He withered away under the heat of the lecherous gaze.

It's a story about a man getting a ground-level view of the objectification generally used to oppress women. It's almost poetic. But the question underlying the story is why the "Untitled" video got such a frenzied response in the first place, and that's because it featured a rare sight: a black man dancing sexually. Contemporary black pop is perhaps more graphically sexual than ever before, but yet there remains a woeful lack of room for black men to express themselves sexually through movement.

The D'Angelo video seems like an odd place to begin a discussion of sexual dance, considering how relatively still D'Angelo's performance is, but it's actually a perfect example of sexual dance.

Broadly, sexual dance is the body moving to music in a way designed to titillate, especially by focusing on specific areas of the male or female anatomy. Movements are austere and usually rhythmic. Sexual dance is done in immodest clothing. Sexual dance emphasizes rapture over technique and form over function and is inherently submissive—designed to invite the lecherous gaze. The dancer tacitly forfeits the right to be viewed as more than a collection of jiggling flesh. Not all male movement associated with sexuality qualifies as sexual dance. For example, the pelvic thrust set to music is not sexual dance. The austerity of movement is there, as is the focus on a specific part of the anatomy, but the submissive quality is lacking. Pelvic thrusting says, "Look what I can do," whereas sexual dance says, "Imagine what you could do with this."

By these standards, most of the dancing seen in black music is not sexual dance. When Chris Brown dances, or Usher or Ne-Yo, there can be a sexual tone, but the dance is too technical, too clean, and too choreographed to be considered sexual dance. It's an expression of showmanship and virtuosity, not sexuality, and it's only sexual in how it evokes the broader idea of black physicality and athleticism. It's a type of movement required of any aspirant to the Michael Jackson template of black pop stardom, and as much spectacular movement as Michael did, very little of it evoked sex.

A prominent, pre-D'Angelo example of hostility toward black male sexual dance is Hammer's infamous 1994 video "Pumps and a Bump," often credited as revitalizing Hammer's career as much as much as it is with destroying it. The video is set in the pool area of Hammer's 40,000-square-foot mansion, which later became a symbol of excess. But the symbol of excess most people were focused on in the "Pumps and a Bump" video was Hammer's package, which bounces around as he gyrates in an indiscreet zebra-print Speedo.

The video was deemed too graphic, amid accusations that Hammer's full erection was on display, and an alternate video was shot with a fully clothed Hammer. The issue came up when he appeared on Arsenio Hall's talk show. Bashful and chastened, Hammer clammed up when Hall asked him to settle the Speedo debate. I interviewed Hammer in 2009, and when I asked about the video, his

D'Angelo in the "Untitled (How Does It Feel)" video.

response was noticeably defensive. He told me men who were uncomfortable with and insecure about seeing him in that swimsuit created the backlash. "The problem was that men weren't interested, but their wives and girl-friends were a little too interested," he said.

A more recent example came this spring, when open-ly gay rapper Fly Young Red released a video for his single "Throw That Boy Pussy," which quickly went viral. The vid-eo is straightforward in its novelty, musically and visually akin to a Soulja Boy video, except that Fly Young Red is gay, hence the big-bootied bodies on display belong to men. The male dancers, clad in tied-off tees and booty shorts, gyrate and twerk while Fly Young Red talks gen-der-flipped shit over the beat: "Clap that ass in a split / Lemme see you clap that ass like a bitch / Yeah I'm trying to get you back home / So I can see you clap that ass on this dick."

The online comment threads on the Fly Young Red vid-eo reflect a wide spectrum of reactions. There's outrage, amusement, support, and some genuine confusion—not to mention a good bit of internal dissent, with gay men debating the video's appropriateness, and expressing a certain level of shame that outsiders were judging their cultural nuances. And of course, there's plenty of religious shame. Perhaps the best comment of the bunch reads, "I just want to let everyone know that if you didn't immedi-ately repent after watching this, it's still not too late to do it now."

There's a narrower range of responses to another vid-eo featuring black men dancing sexually, Sissy Nobby's "Beat It Out the Frame." In one portion of the video, Nobby, who ranks high among the boss bitches of N'awlins sissy bounce, exhorts his male fans to "pop dat dyck up," and they comply, whipping their packages around in silhou-etting mesh shorts.

The relatively muted response to that video has two explanations. First, New Orleans bounce is a music scene with a good amount of sexual fluidity. Second, the afore-mentioned portion is a small part of the video, which ex-cept for that snippet, features twerking black women. So while Sissy Nobby is gay, the "Beat It Out the Frame" vid-eo isn't necessarily gay. It's inclusively sexual. If your thing is watching people sling their mounds to and fro, "Beat It Out the Frame" has something for you. Still, it's worth not-ing that in the online discussion of the video, that small section elicits the most conversation. It's no easy feat to steer a conversation away from a black woman's ass, but the men in Sissy Nobby's video manage to steal the show.

Black men have little room for error when it comes to dancing sexually because that type of movement is not compatible with the way people process black male sexu-ality. Black men's bodies are commodified to the same ex-

It's clear the video has its foundation in the very same rigid, binary ideas of sexuality and gender expression it means to rebel against.

tent that black women's bodies are, but in different ways. Black women are sexually objectified, while black men are sexually weaponized. Black men's sexuality is expected to have physicality, a domination and a brutality that isn't present when a man is dancing sexually by himself. There's room for that when a man and a woman dance together, as it gives the man the opportunity to pulverize his partner with pelvic thrusts in a manner that, while inspired by sex, doesn't resemble actual sex. But for a man, without a partner, to put his body on display through dance requires a level of submission that is as undesirable to black men as it is to their audiences.

There is a reasonable cultural and historical basis for black men resisting this type of dance. There's a deep, painful historical context around black men's bodies being put on display, robbed of their agency, and evaluated exclusively in terms of their function. His strength and his potency can make it difficult for a black man to willingly give in to the urge to shake his ass, which is an acknowledgment of complete submission. To do it with an audience watching is a feat, especially when that audience is expecting something different.

Black men are often complicit in their sexual weaponization. "Beat It Out the Frame" is a perfect example of this, with a sexual overture expressed using violent language and a premium placed on a black man's physicality, stamina, and potency. "Throw That Boy Pussy" is exhilarating and transgressive, but when Fly Young Red specifies that he wants to see you "clap that ass like a bitch," it's clear the video has its foundation in the very same rigid, binary ideas of sexuality and gender expression it means to rebel against.

To the extent black male sexual dance exists, it's often done as mockery of or in tribute to black women's sexual dance, and YouTube is teeming with examples. By couching the dance in irony, black men create a space to enjoy it by distancing themselves from what that type of performance signifies. The ironic stripper performance has become such a common framework through which black men approach sexual dance. That's why so many people had no other way to process the Fly Young Red video other than to assume it was meant to create an absurdly comic effect.

While American culture grows incrementally more accepting of subversions and reinterpretations of sexuality, relationships, and gender identity, attitudes about the sexuality of black bodies seem to have been frozen since 1965. You can fault Miley Cyrus for choosing to surround herself with jiggling black dancers in her recent live shows, but you can't call her inefficient. Cyrus needed to shatter America's wholesome image of her, so she used one of the most incendiary symbols known to man.

That said, black women, just by virtue of existing in a heteronormative culture, have tools of sexual expression in their arsenal that black men don't have. Given the general hostility to black men dancing sexually, it's a dynamic that is unlikely to change soon. That's a shame, given what a potent tool the body can be to undergird the tone or message of a song.

It certainly doesn't help that D'Angelo became a cautionary tale about the dangers of vulnerable, sexual body movement. His story is a fascinating slice of pop psychology, but one that comes with unfortunate subtext. To be black, and to be a man, and to be naked, and to be sexual, and to be submissive, and to be given to rapture, is to know you possess a weapon so powerful, you may never be able to wield it safely. ✐

Joshua Alston is a writer, reporter, and journalist specializing in coverage of arts and culture, politics, race, religion, and gender/sexuality. His work has also been featured in Newsweek, VIBE, Vanity Fair, The Guardian, *and* The A.V. Club. *He lives in Philadelphia.*

Sunflower River Blues

As a teen, guitarist **John Fahey** plunged headlong into the Deep South in search of forgotten blues albums, but found his voice.

BY STEVE LOWENTHAL

When guitarist John Fahey began listening to records, he had no idea what a record collector was. Record collecting was a secret fascination, coded in mailing lists printed in the back of small jazz and record-collector magazines. The most rare and sought-after collectibles sold for hundreds of dollars.

Fahey initially rejected records by black musicians. After record hunting with friend Richard Spottswood, Fahey at first traded the blues records he found in exchange for country records. "Where I was brought up

was very prejudiced toward Negroes," Fahey said. "I was taught to hate and fear them. I didn't like black music very much, I wouldn't even listen to it."

One day, while tallying their scores, Spottswood and Fahey played Blind Willie Johnson's "Praise God I'm Satisfied" to check the record's condition. It was 1957, and what Fahey heard changed him forever. He recalled, "I started to feel nauseated so I made him take it off, but it kept going through my head so I had to hear it again. When he played it the second time I started to cry, it was suddenly very beautiful. It was some kind of hysterical conversion experience where in fact I had liked that kind of music all the time, but didn't want to. So, I allowed myself to like it."

The song tells of a man thanking the Lord for saving him and clearing the clouds away, the joy of religious devotion echoing in Johnson's raspy voice. The music of bluesmen like Charley Patton and Blind Blake—other names he found in similar record scores—sent Fahey spiraling toward more collecting and research. Their guitar playing attracted him, Patton for his energetic and percussive playing and Blake for his sophisticated fingerpicking technique. What they had in common was syncopation.

Fahey related the anger he found in blues music to his own childhood angst. He heard the alienation of outsiders, voices that were ignored and absent from his own world. He felt removed and powerless in the Maryland suburbs and related his own complaints to the blues themes of loneliness and disappointment.

Fahey also found techniques he could use to further develop his guitar language. He taped his favorite records, keeping the recordings for reference and selling the physical records when he could fetch a nice price for them. Like many musicians, he began by studying his idols and playing along to their songs. Among his favorite artists was fingerpicking guitar player Sam McGee, a regular at the Grand Ole Opry known for his lightning-fast playing.

The only way for Fahey to satisfy his emerging need for records was to go out and find them. Searching out old 78s in playable condition became a treasure hunt. There was no other way to hear the original country blues music. Blues music was generally regarded as outdated, no longer of interest to current audiences. To people Fahey's age it was all but unknown. For a handful of young white teens in Maryland, however, it provided a glimpse into another reality, the dark gauze of pops and static only adding to the mystery.

After exhausting their resources locally, Fahey and Spottswood began making long trips from suburban Maryland to the Deep South to find unheard gems, Fahey driving them in his '55 Chevy. Listening to Charley Patton records, they would hear lyrics with the names of towns such as Clarksdale, Mississippi, so they resolved to head to those places to hunt for 78s. Fahey and Spottswood would often canvass poor black neighborhoods. Beyond looking in secondhand stores, the young white men would literally go door to door, looking for dusty old records whose owners no longer wanted them. These requests were such a breach of the racial divide at the time that the residents were wary of the visitors.

About one house in 10 would have some records, and most seemed willing to part with them. Generally they would pay around 25 cents a record. One of Fahey's most valued finds turned out to be the only known existing copy of Charley Patton's "Tom Rushen Blues" / "Pea Vine Blues" on Paramount. An old woman in Clarksdale, Mississippi, agreed to let him into her house and began to play a stack of records, talking about each one. When she reached a Charley Patton record, she began to tell a story about him, as Patton had lived in Clarksdale himself. Fahey cut her off, pretending to be disinterested. He didn't want her to know how much he coveted the record. He badgered her into a sale, wanting to abscond with his treasure before she could reconsider. Fahey, overwhelmed by his good fortune, gloated about his discovery.

His sympathies and politics were naïve, and they remained undeveloped despite his repeated trips to the South. All he saw was the music; the realities of poverty and institutionalized racism were far from his mind. Fixated on the musical expressions of the underclass, he expressed no regrets about their condition. Fahey acted as if he were myopically concerned with music, playing up his tough-guy image to his friends with provocative racist comments. But this front masked fear rather than hatred. The hardships of the impoverished and ignored, as represented through the records, spoke to him more than he was ready to admit.

After unearthing a few major discoveries, Fahey and his friends became sellers, buyers, and traders in an obscure world. There were only a handful of collectors in the DC metro area and they had come to know each other quite well. Spottswood was more interested in collecting than selling, amassing a gigantic catalog of pre-war American music. "Today we have a pretty good idea of the breadth and scope of the commercial sound recordings of the 1920s, but in those days we were still discovering things," recalls Spottswood. "I would stockpile everything, but John would turn around and sell them if he needed money."

To cement his reputation and better capitalize on his finds, occasionally Fahey destroyed extremely rare records he found but which he already had, just to

The only way for Fahey to satisfy his emerging need for records was to go out and find them. Searching out old 78s in playable condition became a treasure hunt. There was no other way to hear the original country blues music.

make his own copy more valuable. It was an act of self-ishness he'd later regret. Fahey would often sell records to subsidize his canvassing trips. The records were auctioned by mail, after being strictly graded for condition, through private mailing lists. He had many buyers in New York, at least three of whom formed a record label, the Origin Jazz Library, which started reissuing compilation albums of songs from old 78s in 1962. Notably, they introduced Skip James's "Devil Got My Woman" to a new audience on their *Really! The Country Blues 1927–1933* collection.

Spottswood's Zen calm was the inverse of Fahey's wild enthusiasm. "The records represented the art and that was the only way you could experience it," Spottswood says. "There weren't any people playing this music anymore. It was the only way to access the sound of a generation that had already passed. We white kids were experiencing them for the first time, because our parents had ignored that music totally." Though there had been research into the vast numbers of 78s pressed in earlier decades, many discoveries still remained to be made. The excitement of the unknown propelled Fahey and Spottswood forward.

Fahey heard in the blues a rage not expressed elsewhere, and stories fascinated with death, violence, and sex. "The reason I liked Charley Patton and those other Delta singers so much was because they were angry," Fahey remembered. "Their music is ominous. Patton had a rheumatic heart, and he knew that he was going to die young, which he did. In Son House you hear a lot of fear. In Skip James you hear a lot of sorrow, but also a lot of anger."

Fahey started to incorporate blues techniques and melodic fragments into his own guitar work. With his heavy thumb he alternated the bass on the sixth and fourth or fifth and third strings of the guitar while his middle and ring fingers picked out a melody. He then would use bent notes and slides to mimic the vocal

phrasings of the blues. This combination gave his playing a richly dynamic sound, with lead, rhythm, and melody all incorporated into a single instrumental performance. Though Blind Blake, Sam McGee, and Mississippi John Hurt all utilized similar techniques, Fahey fused them with his interest in dissonant modernism, taking his music somewhere else entirely.

Back at home, Fahey and Spottswood would make frequent trips to visit fellow country and blues collector Joe Bussard, another collector of the same age who lived in nearby Frederick. Along with various other collectors, they would hang out in Bussard's basement, listen to records, and trade their finds. Few young people had similar tastes, so Fahey, Bussard, and Spottswood enjoyed the chance to share with each other and talk shop.

By that time, home electronics had also emerged as a hobby, and many kids in the '50s built their own transistor radios. Bussard made a lathe cutting machine at home and cut records one at a time from his basement. He'd even draw his own center labels by hand. Bussard greatly admired Fahey's guitar playing and asked to record him. He instructed Fahey to sing as rough as he could—so he would sound like a real bluesman. On these early home recordings, Fahey is heard singing far off key. As a singer, he seems hesitant and affected, as if trying to sound more withered and aged, or at other times simply laconic, covering songs by his newfound idol Charley Patton like "Some Summer Day."

Under the pseudonym Blind Thomas, Fahey cut six sides for Bussard's personal Fonotone label. For the most part, the recordings were just for fun. The actual market for such 78s was microscopic, as Bussard primarily did trades through the mail with other collectors and obsessive types. He also hosted a bluegrass radio show, on which he sold his Fonotone records for one dollar each on the air. Fahey, too, loved the idea of fooling some hopeless collector. That was the cover at

^
FAHEY WITH TORTOISE

John and Jan Fahey enjoying a London vacation, 1969.

PHOTO COURTESY OF THE COLLECTION OF JAN LEBOW FAHEY

least; but underneath the joke a more serious desire began brewing. Fahey always insisted that the recordings were inferior, never meant to be released, and never meant much to him. However, there are traces of what would become his seminal style, a heavy thumb keeping the rhythm and a richly melodic sense with minimal embellishments.

The Fonotone recordings provide a template for the American Primitive style and are also an early example of a private press record label, a concept that came to greater fruition decades later. Knowing no one would be interested in their goings-on, the pressure was off Fahey and Bussard, and the records were made largely for their own enjoyment. But Fahey found a voice for himself through this process.

In 1960, Fahey entered his first year at the University of Maryland at College Park. He then quickly transferred to American University in Washington, DC, where he studied religion and philosophy, both natural fits for his aptitudes. "He had gotten his degree in philosophy at American University and he did some hard and honest work there," says Spottswood. "John was someone who had anti-intellectual tendencies but he was fairly intellectual." By then he had ditched his

teen tough-guy act and started to ease up on his friends. "He had matured dramatically," recalls Lee. "He had stopped hanging around with a pack of half-witted, socially misfit punks, had been accepted as an intellectual equal by the adults at St. Michael's, and had begun to be recognized musically. So, having a more secure sense of himself, he began treating me more decently."

Fahey continued collecting records, and socialized, drank, and played music with his friends. He and Spottswood at times played guitar and harmonica respectively at college parties in DC. Fahey often played with his back against the door so no one could leave the room while they were performing. This activity was at first purely recreational, but Fahey soon found something more to propel him. ✎

Excerpted with permission from *Dance of Death: The Life of John Fahey, American Guitarist* by Steve Lowenthal. Published by Chicago Review Press, June 2014.

Steve Lowenthal started and ran the music magazine Swingset. *His writing has also been published in* Fader, SPIN, Vice, *and the* Village Voice. *He ran the record label Plastic for five years and currently runs the VDSQ label, which specializes in solo instrumental acoustic guitar music. He lives in New York City.*

F A N S

CURATED BY CHRISTIAN STORM

Ryan McGinley *You & My Friends (Worldwide), 2014*

Debra Friedman Deadheads, Rich Stadium, Buffalo, New York, 1989

Daniel Cronin The Gathering of the Juggalos, Cave-In-Rock, Illinois, 2010

Jem Cohen From the film *Instrument*, 1999

Melchior Tersen Nicki Manaj, Paris, France, 2012

Melchior Tersen Motörhead, Paris, France, 2012

Ryan Mastro Bonnaroo, Manchester, Tennessee, 2012

Noah Sheldon Midi Festival, Century Park in Pudong New Area, Shanghai, China, 2011

Cheryl Dunn Moby, B4BC Music Festival, Sierra-at-Tahoe Resort, California, 1997

Tim Barber Kendrick Lamar, ØYA Fest, Oslo, Norway, 2013

Boogie New York, New York, December, 2008

Jörg Brüggemann Summer Night Open Air Festival, Mining am Inn, Austria, 2009

Chad Moore *Meghan*, Mercury Lounge, New York, New York, 2012

Cheryl Dunn Thompson Square Park Riots 30th Anniversary concert, New York, New York, 2008

Michael Jang The Dils, San Francisco Art Institute, 1978

David C. Sampson Pitchfork Music Festival, Chicago, Illinois, 2012

Julian Gilbert Nassau Coliseum, Uniondale, New York, 2009

Jamel Shabazz Dave Chappelle block party, Bed-Stuy, Brooklyn, New York, 2006

David C. Sampson Pitchfork Music Festival, Chicago, Illinois, 2012

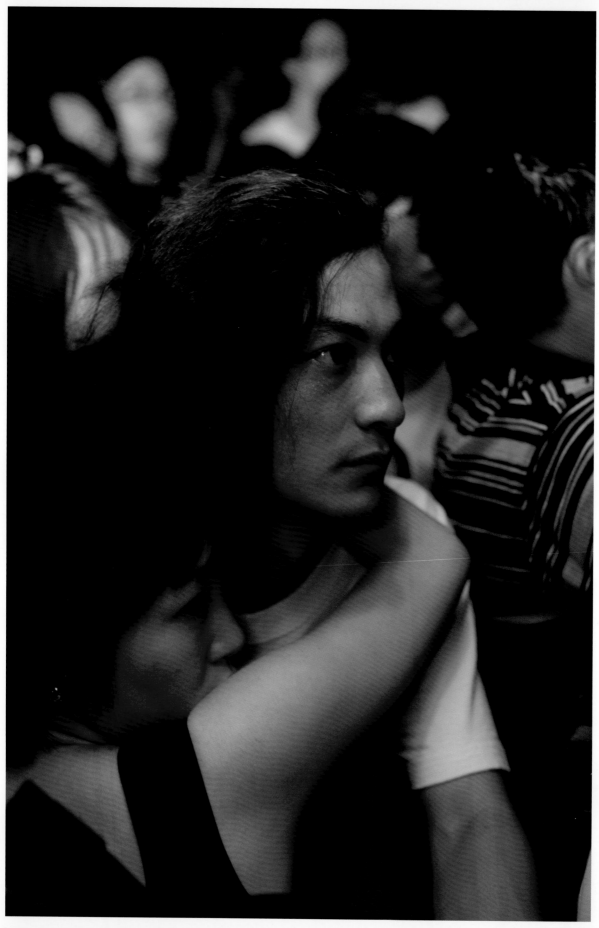

Wolfgang Tillmans Fans at a Concert, 2009

Steve Perille August Jam, Charlotte Motor Speedway, Concord, North Carolina, 1974

Jörg Brüggemann Legacy Festival, Dessau, Germany, 2009

Paley Fairman Coachella, Indio, California, 2013

Melchior Tersen Hellfest, Paris, France, 2011

Control P

Control P is the section of *The Pitchfork Review* where we take a look back at and expand some of our favorite pieces from Pitchfork.com, adding bonus content and insights from our writers and readers. This time we revisit the comprehensive oral history of Elliott Smith, our hashtagged world, a classic Rolling On Dubs installment, if *Sung Tongs* is embarrassing or not, and gaze upon St. Vincent.

Keep the Things You Forgot: An Elliott Smith Oral History

By Jayson Greene

PHOTOGRAPHS BY AUTUMN DE WILDE

Ten years after Elliott Smith's death, nearly 20 people who knew him talk to Jayson Greene about the singer/ songwriter's remarkable musical legacy, album by album.

Ever since he died, one decade ago, people have been clamoring to tell Elliott Smith's story for him: writers, poets, fellow musicians, his religiously devoted fans—anyone who felt the subliminal undertow of his songs. The urge is understandable. Smith's music, with its forensic attention to mood, dredges some of our murkiest emotions to the surface and coaxes unnameable sensations into focus. When an artist has this gift, they stir powerful needs.

Since the moment Smith began making solo recordings, beginning with the whispered, hyper-intimate 1994 collection *Roman Candle*, he has inspired fervent reactions. His story is dotted with followers, people who instinctively grasped the appeal of his music and felt themselves helplessly conscripted to his cause. They became storytellers for Elliott's genius and originality, champions for someone allergic to championing himself.

What follows is not an oral history of his life, but of his music; specifically, his solo career. The lines between life and music are tangled, of course, in ways that aren't neatly prizable, and darker stories eventually creep into the frame at the edges. But the arc traced here begins with the emergence of that voice: the flowering of his talent, the development of the intimate, inscrutable folk-pop he would mine for the rest of his career.

That discovery dovetails with the dissolution of his first band, the loud-rocking Heatmiser. In some ways the development of the former triggered the latter. The story told here begins at this hinge point, as Smith begins exploring the possibilities of his fiercely intimate four-track solo recordings that would pull him away from Heatmiser and, eventually, into the national spotlight.

For those who knew him personally, the task of speaking for Elliott Smith wavers between privilege and burden. Many of the 18 people who spoke to me—bandmates, producers, managers, friends—emerged hesitantly, stepping gingerly over their own profound misgivings, issuing grave caveats. They'd been burned before, they warned me. They swore they'd never speak again. The story of their self-imposed silence, and their individual choices to break it or hold it, runs in powerful counterpoint to Smith's own story. Some of the singer's closest associates have simply declined to go on record. Having been prodded multiple times, they have understandably snapped shut. Some are speaking now for the first time. The combination of profound ambivalence and fierce conviction in their voices, as they opened themselves up, was chastening.

HEATMISER

In 1984, Elliott Smith—born Steven Paul Smith—moves to Portland from Duncanville, Texas, to live with his father, Gary Smith, and Gary's wife Marta Greenwald. There, at Lincoln High School, he meets Tony Lash, future drummer of Heatmiser, and forms his first band, Stranger Than Fiction. Upon graduating, he goes off to Hampshire College in Amherst, Massachusetts, where he meets Neil Gust and forms an early version of Heatmiser. (It is around this time that Steven Paul Smith begins going by "Elliott.") When he returns to Portland after graduation, Smith forms the final Heatmiser lineup along with Gust, Lash, and bassist Brandt Peterson.

TONY LASH [*high school friend; drummer, Heatmiser*]: In the high school band, I played flute and Elliott played clarinet. He was funny, and we were both kind of nerdy. A friend of mine introduced us because we both liked Rush.

Elliott's songs were ridiculously complicated then. He had so many ideas, and he hadn't really developed

his arrangement skills, so the songs would start in one place and go through all these sections and then end arbitrarily. But having come from a prog background, it wasn't hard for me to negotiate all the time changes. We recorded our one really ambitious album when I was a senior and he was a junior; we definitely aimed high, even if the results weren't necessarily stellar.

We kept in touch while he was at Hampshire College. I stayed in Portland and went into record production, getting a job at a studio. Every summer we worked on some kind of a project. Then Elliott came back from college, and we started playing together again as Heatmiser.

JJ GONSON [*manager, Heatmiser; girlfriend*]: The first time I saw Heatmiser was in 1993, at X-Ray in Portland. I had this visceral response, which I've only had with a few bands. I was impressed by every single member. Elliott was clearly an über-talented songwriter. Neil [Gust] was clearly an almost-as-talented songwriter. And they both had terrific singing voices and were really gifted guitar players. The drummer [Tony Lash] was excellent. There was not a slacker in Heatmiser.

Neil and Elliott had very different guitar skills that complemented each other beautifully. In fact, when I met them, I would say that Neil was the more accomplished of the two. But Elliott had a natural aptitude that was unique. He could hear music and make it come out of his fingers in a way that most guitar players can't. He never stumbled. It was like there was a channel that went straight from his brain to his fingers, and that was immediately evident watching him play live. You only see that kind of skill level once in a while, so when you see it, you know it.

JJ GONSON: A phenomenal thing happened in Portland in the early '90s. At La Luna, someone had this idea to charge one dollar at the door to see three local bands every Monday night. The club capacity was maybe a thousand, and they got to keep the bar, but the bands could sell merchandise, and they got 100% of the door. So every Monday night the bands were pretty much guaranteed at least $300—which was huge in 1993—and the shows had Heatmiser, Crackerbash, Pond, Hazel, and The Dandy Warhols. It was all local. It sold out every Monday because nobody had a job, really—this was the early '90s and there was no work. The bands would get their cash, and more importantly, they

"I put it on and their jaws dropped. They released it without changing a thing. That's *Roman Candle*."

—JJ Gonson

would have the experience of playing in front of a thousand people who knew their songs. What you ended up with were these bands that performed *really well*.

Heatmiser was just a phenomenal, rip-your-head-off-and-shove-it-up-your-ass rock band. I saw them hundreds of times. Elliott was so into it; in every photo I took of them onstage from that time, he's biting his lip. The thing I remember most vividly is that he always had this exact same rocking motion in his body language.

ROMAN CANDLE (1994)

In 1993, Smith moves in with JJ Gonson, at a house on Southeast 29th Avenue and Taylor Street in Portland. In the basement, he begins rehearsing and recording the music that would become his first solo release, Roman Candle.

JJ GONSON: For a long time we were "just good friends," and I remember seeing him leaning against an ex-girlfriend one time and thinking, "Why is that bothering me? That shouldn't be bothering me." I'd already worked with the band for awhile, and he wrote songs about feeling like he shouldn't be dating me, wanting to, and knowing that it wasn't the right thing to do. Neither of us would deal with it for a long time. And when we finally did, all of our friends were like, "No! That's a really bad idea!" [*laughs*] Was it a bad idea? I don't know. He was the love of my life in a lot of ways. I'm enormously grateful to have had that emotional experience. I think that everybody should be *that* in love with somebody, even if it has to come to an end.

At the Taylor Street house, he would sit upstairs playing for hours and hours and hours, working on the songs, and then he'd go downstairs for half an hour and put something down on tape. He didn't spend very much time in the "studio," which was the basement. It was gross down there.

The whole sound quality of *Roman Candle* is entirely based on the fact that he's using a low-quality microphone right up against his fingers. He doesn't even have an acoustic pickup—he's playing an acoustic guitar into a microphone.

I had a copy of the finished cassette on me all the time, and I was listening to it all the time. I had a lot of friends at Sub Pop and Matador and Cavity Search and all these record labels, and I was hanging out with them because I was promoting [Heatmiser], and I needed these labels to put their bands on tour with my band, but I didn't burst into Cavity Search Records like, "You have to play this! It's the best thing you've ever heard, and you need to release it right now." I was probably just like, "I've got this solo cassette by Elliott." "What? Elliott does solo stuff?" I put it on and their jaws dropped. They released it without changing a thing. That's *Roman Candle*.

TONY LASH: We mixed *Roman Candle* in my basement—to the extent that you can mix off of a four-track cassette. It was so different from what Heatmiser was doing. I didn't have a sense right then that it was going to become this big thing. A lot more care was taken with recording his second solo record, but even then it seemed more like an extremely viable side project to me, with Heatmiser as the main focus.

SLIM MOON [*founder, Kill Rock Stars*]: I didn't know Elliott at all, but we were both playing on this small tour of solo artists going down the West Coast. The first night was in Seattle, and I missed Elliott's set. The second night was at the Bottom of the Hill in San Francisco, and I was blown away by Elliott's set. So I went out to the car to listen to [*Roman Candle*] rather than staying for the rest of the show.

The song that blew me away was "Last Call." It's in my top 10 favorite songs to this day. It's the perfect song in terms of lyrics, melody, as a piece of poetry: "You're a crisis / You're an icicle / You're a tongueless talker / You

"I was blown away by Elliott's set. So I went out to the car to listen to [*Roman Candle*] rather than staying for the rest of the show." —Slim Moon

don't care what you say / You're a jaywalker and you just walk away." Those lines stick with me.

There's this little trick that he does in that song where he drops the tuning at the end. It almost feels like it's two songs edited together, except he would play it live and reach over and just turn the tuning peg as he played. It's not a studio trick. It impressed me that it was all done on a four-track, too, because the cheaper the production is, the less you can hide your flaws.

LARRY CRANE [*owner, Jackpot! Recording Studio; producer/engineer; archivist for Smith's family*]: I'm really supportive of the local music scene and everything, but I'm not always impressed by the quality of other people's work. [*laughs*] But when I heard *Roman Candle*, I thought, "Wow, that's pretty good for the guy from Heatmiser." Initially, I thought Heatmiser was another crummy, wild guitar band that the grunge era brought up. But I started realizing, "Oh wait, they have songs."

MARGARET MITTLEMAN [*manager*]: Slim Moon fell in love with Elliott, and he told me I had to come down and see him. I don't remember what he played. I'm more of a vibe person, and Elliott's demeanor hit me right away, right in the stomach. He was just sitting in a chair in the corner, but he seemed so special in every way.

We talked after that show. My intent was just to help him. He wasn't interested in a publishing contract or a manager. I was working at BMG Publishing, and one of our goals at the time was to sign things really inexpensively and just offer services. Anyway, he liked us, and he liked that we had done work with Beck, who was a recent artist I had signed. We developed a friendship.

ELLIOTT SMITH (1995)

Smith records his self-titled record at friend Leslie Uppinghouse's house, moving on from Cavity Search to Slim Moon's Kill Rock Stars label. The album is released on July 21, 1995, accompanied by a larger promotional campaign.

SLIM MOON: We talked about his ideas or hopes for the next step after *Roman Candle*, and he mentioned that he was interested in being on K Records. I knew [K owner] Calvin [Johnson], so over the next couple of months, I gave him a copy of the record, told him that Elliott was the real deal, and told him to come see him play. I never heard back from Calvin about that. To my knowledge, Elliott never heard from Calvin either. I talked to Elliott a while later and said, "Would it be cool if Kill Rock Stars put out a 7-inch?"

We never did multi-record deals at Kill Rock Stars back then. We would just do one album, see how it went, and then discuss it again. Before we put out *Elliott Smith*, I looked at SoundScan, and it showed that half of the sales of *Roman Candle* had been in Portland, and he was basically unknown everywhere else. I figured that if anyone could be wildly popular in one town, then that could be replicated everywhere, all you have to do is get the word out. But *Elliott Smith* really didn't sell that well.

JJ GONSON: It was embarrassing to be doing acoustic music. Nobody did it. Everybody was rough. There was no pop going on at that time. Elliott and I used to play Peter, Paul and Mary, The Beatles, and Captain and Tennille covers together in the bedroom with the door closed, hoping nobody could hear us. I will never forget Neil laughing the first time Elliott played him a solo song, the part where his voice goes up on "No Name #1." *Laughing*. It was just shocking.

I can't *not* acknowledge the fact that we are talking here about Portland, Oregon, in the '90s. This was O.H.—Original Hipster—so you had a lot of deeply ironic listening material, like whale songs, or Halloween Sound Effects records, or Tito Puente, or some Spanish movie soundtrack.

MARGARET MITTLEMAN: I remember one night we did karaoke with [Sleater-Kinney/Quasi's] Janet [Weiss] and [Smith bandmate] Sam [Coomes], and me and Janet did "Ride Captain Ride" together. Elliott might have done Rush.

ROB SCHNAPF [*producer,* Heatmiser's Mic City Sons, *along with* Either/Or, XO, *and* Figure 8; *married to Margaret Mittleman*]: He actually did "Rock You Like a Hurricane" by the Scorpions. The look on Elliott's face when he realized how high Klaus Meine's voice is on that first note—the realization of having miscalculated in public with a microphone in your hand—oh, it was good.

JJ GONSON: He would walk up behind me and put his arms around me and sing [the Carpenters'] "(They Long to Be) Close to You" to me. At one point when we were falling apart, he made me a beautiful cassette recording of the Cheap Trick song "If You Want My Love." I wish I knew where it was, but I don't.

MARGARET MITTLEMAN: When I would tell the other bands I was working with that I was working with Elliott Smith, they'd be like, "Oh, why? That's weird." Eventually, of course, they became his biggest fans.

Between 1994 and 1996, Smith tours regularly as a solo artist while remaining the co-frontman of Heatmiser.

SLIM MOON: A couple of the shows we played on that *Roman Candle* tour in 1994 were really poorly promoted, so we'd goof off, and Elliott would play a lot of Hank Williams and stuff.

MARGARET MITTLEMAN: Elliott's first solo tour on the East Coast was painful because he was still becoming comfortable with performing alone—and not just alone, but alone to an empty room. He was nervous about it, and it used to make him ... not feel good a lot. He dealt with a lot of stomach issues. So I'd always be the one telling him, "You can do it." But whether it would be one person or five, somebody inevitably would discover him from that one experience, and the next time he went back, it was easier.

ROB SCHNAPF: He used to play these shows and he wouldn't finish songs and he would just kind of give up, and Margaret would be like, "Nope, you're gonna go out there, you've gotta finish your songs, go back up the stairs." He'd say, "What if someone's talking?" And she'd say, "Who cares? You wanna do this, right? Well, this is what you've gotta do. You're gonna be playing this bowling alley in Nebraska next. Good luck."

MARY LOU LORD: [*singer/songwriter; tourmate; KRS labelmate*]: Slim really liked this kid. We were all together on a bill; me, Slim, and Elliott. I was backstage, just talking to everybody, and Slim said, "Mary Lou, you really need to go out and watch that guy." I wasn't very interested; I had heard a million acoustic guitar guys, you know? But Slim was like, "No, Mary Lou, you *really* need to go and watch him." In other words, "Shut the fuck up and get out there."

The first thing I noticed was that his guitar was really crappy; I think it might have been the Le Domino he recorded *Roman Candle* on. I realized he was making that crappy guitar sound really good. By the third song, I had completely lost myself. I was sucked in. I immediately invited him on tour. And he mumbled, in his way, "Okay, Mary Lou."

LOU BARLOW [*frontman, Sebadoh*]: He opened solo for Sebadoh in '96, and it was at a time when no one really knew about him. We were at our peak at that point, and people just talked right through his set. It would make me really angry. I'd be like, "What the hell are you doing talking through his set? It's Elliott Smith! He's great!" I had that feeling like, "Someday you idiots will shut up and listen to him." I remember telling him, "People won't shut up, It's making me so angry." And he's like, "I like it better this way. It makes me less self-conscious."

STEVEN DROZD [*drummer/multi-instrumentalist, The Flaming Lips*]: I met Elliott in '96. I was on that Sebadoh tour with Those Bastard Souls. I was very intimidated by him when I first met him. He just seemed like such a fucking serious dude. He was kind of a nobody back then, but he already had something about him. Between him and Lou Barlow, I was pretty struck. I treaded lightly.

REBECCA GATES [*singer/guitarist, The Spinanes*]: We toured together for [The Spinanes'] *Strand* in 1996. I would never really sit down and play, except for during soundcheck and shows, but when we showed up anywhere, Elliott would just start playing guitar, whether he was writing, or practicing, or just playing covers. It wasn't like, "Here I am, check me out!" It was just to himself. He was someone who was always thinking about songwriting.

MARY LOU LORD: We both applied to South By Southwest around 1995, and we got turned down. So I said, "Elliott, who are those assholes to tell us we can't play?" I had this little busking amp I kept in my car at all times, just in case. So we drove down there and found a little place to play near the Driskill Hotel. I kind of wore the pants on that tour [laughs], and Elliott was like, "I don't know about this, Mary Lou." And I was like, "That's enough outta you. We're going to have our own little showcase out in front of this Kinko's."

We got a bunch of booze and started playing. I wish to god somebody had recorded this because it was St. Patrick's Day and Elliott was playing all kinds of Irish songs and Pogues songs. We'd take turns, and we played all night and got happily shit-faced. The people who actually had a showcase at Kill Rock Stars came by; Slim was there. It was one of the best nights of my life.

MIKE DOUGHTY [frontman, Soul Coughing]: I saw Elliott in New York with the Magnetic Fields on the same bill. No one had heard of either of them. It was *literally* a life-changing show. I was like, "I don't want to do Soul Coughing anymore. I want to do this—when I grow up, I want to be this man." I went out the next day to whatever groovy-people record store was closest and bought *Roman Candle* and *Elliott Smith*.

The thing that I always keep in mind is the hiss from the tape on *Elliott Smith*. Those are not sounds that an engineer would be particularly proud of. And there's a lyric from "Christian Brothers" that I want to put up in neon across the length of Metropolitan Avenue in Brooklyn: "No bad dream fucker's gonna boss me around." I'm getting chills right now just saying that.

LOU BARLOW: I related to him in a lot of ways because when he was in the zone of performing acoustically, he was just hunched over. I mean, the guy didn't really ever look up. There was none of this, "I'm a performer," you know? Almost no acknowledgement. There was almost an *anger* that I really related to.

I remember he was soundchecking in Philadelphia at the Theatre of Living Arts. I would always watch his soundchecks, so I was sitting there, and he covered "Thirteen" by Big Star. It just brought me to tears. Music doesn't always bring me to tears; if I hear "Love" by John Lennon at a vulnerable moment it will bring me to tears. His version of "Thirteen" was devastating in that empty theater. I don't think he even knew I was there.

DORIEN GARRY [*friend, publicist at Girlie Action Media*]: I first met him around 1995, when I was 17 or 18 and working the door at Maxwell's. It was a Sunday night, and he was on tour with The Softies. Not very many people showed up to the gig. None of those guys had a place to stay, and I lived in kind of a halfway house for musicians in Jersey City at the time, so they stayed there for the night.

Totally coincidentally, within the next six months or so, I got hired at Girlie Action to do publicity and I worked for him. I handled the college fanzine stuff, and we became pretty close during that short span of time. That was such a different time in the music industry. There was no internet; fanzines were our internet—and using the post office was our information superhighway, I guess. [*laughs*]

Because we were friends, he was able to tell me what he was and wasn't comfortable with. The more attention he got, the more troubled he got, and that's when it got hard. The irony of it was that he was so open and honest with pretty much anybody who crossed his path, so it wasn't unlike him to tell a very personal, private story to a virtual stranger sitting next to him at a bar.

But it would infuriate him when people asked him what his lyrics were about. He really hated having to have an answer for what every character and every story was. I mean, "Needle in the Hay" is obviously about drugs and despair. But I when I got to know him better, I learned that song was more about what was going on in the Pacific Northwest in the small music community in the early '90s, and how badly drugs were infiltrating it.

JJ GONSON: It always surprised me what pictures of mine he loved. That one of people falling that's on the front of *Elliott Smith*—he loved that one, and I wouldn't have even noticed it.

REBECCA GATES: When I sang backup vocals on "St. Ides Heaven," he was so focused on how he wanted things to sound. I have a weird way of singing harmonies sometimes, and I just remember him remarking on that: "Ah, I wouldn't have gone for that note, but it works great." Maybe this has shifted now with digital recording, but the one thing that was really special about having those chances to record back then was

that it didn't happen all the time. It was this really lovely space that you created.

LOU BARLOW: When I would play Elliott's music in the house, my wife at the time was pissed. She was like, "This sounds like Sebadoh! It sounds like your acoustic stuff!" She was just livid about it. I couldn't really hear it, though; I heard much more of a folk tradition with him, and his music was more elaborate, where my stuff tended to be simpler.

EITHER/OR (1997)

Either/Or, Smith's final album for Kill Rock Stars, is released on February 25, 1997. Portions of it are recorded at his then girlfriend Joanna Bolme's house; at Mary Lou Lord's home studio; and in the basement of engineer/producer Larry Crane. Smith and Crane, after becoming friends, go on to build and open Jackpot! Recording Studio.

LARRY CRANE: I kind of knew who Elliott was through Joanna [Bolme] because she worked at La Luna. We were throwing some random party, and everyone was sitting around the backyard having a barbecue. Joanna and Elliott were there, and that's when I first remember showing them my home studio, and Elliott saying, "Oh, I have the same tape deck as you. Maybe I could come over here and do some vocals over that." The next thing I know, we were tracking the vocals for "Pictures of Me." When we recorded that song, I remember turning to him and saying, "Oh, you like The Zombies?"

We both wanted to go in on a studio together. I had this beat-up little Toyota pickup and we'd drive around Portland just looking through "For Rent" signs, listening to Simon & Garfunkel and The Left Banke. When we moved into the Jackpot! space and started building it, we had a boom box with CDs and cassettes, and we listened to all kinds of stuff: Television, The Saints. The only thing that drove him crazy was my obsession with Petula Clark. It didn't really dawn on me for quite awhile that we were becoming friends. We opened Jackpot! in February, 1997.

Recording sessions were never really long and drawn out with him. Just three or four hours. If it wasn't going the right way, he'd say, "Make a rough mix of it for me, and let's go get a drink." Back then, it felt more like college than work. There was also a lot of silly stuff. A friend dropped off a Casio guitar made out of rubber, and I was supposed to give it to someone but I kept it around. And Elliott *loved* that thing. He would always strap it on and play, like, Stevie Wonder's "Superstition." You can actually hear it on "Bled White." It makes a *neener-wheeee* sound. He decided he had to bring it to L.A. to show Jon Brion.

DORIEN GARRY: We watched *All That Jazz* together once. It was the rare night where I convinced him to stay home with me and not go out. We both loved it. The main character, who wreaks havoc on this dance community, is wearing this black leather armband. Halfway through the movie, Elliott's like, "I really like that huge bracelet thing." I'm like, "Yeah, it's pretty badass." And then the next day he's like, "Do you know where I can go get a scrap of leather?" So that's basically where the whole leather armband trend of the '90s came from—Elliott seeing *All That Jazz.*

LARRY CRANE: We recorded a lot of cool stuff just incidentally. Someone would always be milling about, and then he'd just say, "Hey, can you help me track this?" That's actually how "Miss Misery" came about. He laid down the instrumental and then made a cassette of it. And then at some point he came back from out of town and said, "Hey, play us that one song." And I'm like, "Which one?" But we put it up, and he put all the vocals on it that day.

Whenever we did an early version of a song, he would say, "I need to send out a probe." So we'd leave a track open just for him to hear and sing along. He would look for the notes that needed harmonies, and then we'd roll the tape, and he'd sing them. He was obsessive about stuff like that. When we were tracking vocals for "Pictures of Me," I was amazed how many layers he built up. The music was all on two tracks, and the other six tracks ended up being vocals. I was like, "That's a little excessive!" [*laughs*]

I've seen very few people who are solo multi-instrumentalist artists who can really work that way. It was very much like a Brian Wilson thing where he locked in. He would be playing a song on guitar and then he'd say, "Maybe this would be better on piano." And in a split second he walks over and starts playing it on piano.

ROB SCHNAPF: We recorded "Between the Bars," "Angeles," and "Say Yes" at [Schnapf and Rothrock's Hum-boldt County, California, studio] the Shop. He would record one live take of vocal and guitar together, and then he would just double it once we got it. It was just absurd. The guitar stuff isn't easy. It was ridiculous that he was able to just nail a vocal and guitar performance live, and he was able to double it live again. I mean, it's not like he's strumming G-C-D. There are intricate little fills. It sounds so natural, and so simple—then *you* try to play it. And sing at the same time. He was just *really* good. Understated, but really good.

LUKE WOOD [*DreamWorks A&R*]: The most available example of Elliott's skill as a writer, and his way with metaphor, is probably "Between the Bars." It works on three layers. It's about love, at first, or it seems to be; you could look at it literally, being about going out for a night out at the bars; the imagery could easily be about prison; and, of course, it's potentially about addiction. The clarity and continuity of thought is amazing—he can take a metaphor like that and sing about it for three minutes and never leave.

JJ GONSON: He recorded *Either/Or* partly at my studio, which was a funny thing because, at that point, we weren't actually speaking to each other. But for months, he was next door to where I worked, so I could hear all these songs being made because my office shared a wall with where he was recording. It was hell. Good songs, though. *Really* good songs.

That was around the time he was breaking away from Heatmiser. It's too bad, he wasn't actually aware that you could have a conversation with somebody and say, "Look, I want to do some music that isn't Heatmiser, so I want to do this." Instead, he would just shut down and not say anything. So it was all done in this very underhanded way. I don't want to be disparaging of him, but this is just unfortunately how he operated. And then when we split up, I kept trying to juggle his solo career with the band, but I didn't have any communication at that point because he wouldn't let me talk to his manager [Margaret Mittleman].

Tony [Lash] and I were like, "We just have to keep it friendly, keep moving, get [the Heatmiser] record done." Because they had signed a contract with Virgin Records, and they had obligations to fulfill. They were supposed to be supporting a record, so they booked a tour, and then Elliott bailed, as I recall. We're like, "What?!" This was after he and I had broken up, and he

"The look on Elliott's face when he realized how high Klaus Meine's voice is on that first note—the realization of having miscalculated in public with a microphone in your hand—oh, it was good."

—Rob Schnapf

---

said, "I am prioritizing my solo career over the band." It was pretty shocking to everyone because the band had worked really hard for a number of years. It could have been both.

TONY LASH: It was almost mid-tour with Heatmiser when he really wanted to change up the sound of the band. This might've been the genesis of the struggles between the two of us because I was resistant to that, but it was mostly because, as a drummer, I liked playing rock stuff; playing quieter music wasn't really my strong point back then, so I was hesitant. He was immediately frustrated. During that whole time, I remember enjoying playing concerts less, but thinking the music was a lot better.

LOU BARLOW: Somehow, we ended up doing the overnight drive from Phoenix to San Diego together in his car when we were touring together. We just talked the whole time, and that was probably the closest I got to him at that point. At that time in Sebadoh, I was like, "I gotta kick the drummer out. This sucks. He's a really good friend." He'd had some issues moving forward from Heatmiser because those were his buds, and going solo was a big change for him. We discussed changing and sometimes leaving your friends behind for the sake of moving forward creatively and artistically. He was a really smart guy.

On the cover of *Either/Or*, he's standing in front of this mirror, and I was there the night that picture was taken. Our tour manager took that picture, and she also took an identical picture of Sebadoh, with the exact same angle. I've gotta find that somewhere.

MARGARET MITTLEMAN: When he opened for Mark Eitzel from American Music Club at Brownies in New York in '97, he finally got the room to be quiet. That was the big challenge. There was this core audience that would sit up front and be quiet, but at the bar people would be talking, and the cash register would be going. There was a Troubadour show where people asked the bar not to ring up anything on the cash register during his set. You could hear a pin drop. That was the first time I remember the vibe being different. People weren't just there to see this next big thing. It was, "I need to see this guy."

XO (1998)

In 1997, Elliott Smith is bought out of his Virgin contract by DreamWorks. He settles into Sunset Sound, on Sunset Boulevard—the studio where The Rolling Stones' Exile on Main Street, Led Zeppelin II *and* IV, *and Beck's* Odelay *were recorded, among others—with producers Rob Schnapf and Tom Rothrock to begin sessions for* XO, *his DreamWorks debut.*

LENNY WARONKER [*DreamWorks co-CEO*]: Tom [Rothrock] and Rob [Schnapf] came to see me when we first started DreamWorks. They played us Elliott Smith, among other things. It was something from *Either/Or*, I think, and I said, "What the hell is *that*?" Just the sound of his double-tracked voice and the acoustic guitar was so unique—maybe there was some George Harrison in there, but what he was doing was uniquely his. And they said, "No, that's not available."

It was pretty much predetermined that he was gonna move from Heatmiser, but there was still the Virgin/Capitol part, and Elliott had to sort of do that himself. He had a contractual obligation there, both as Heatmiser and as a solo artist. I had a meeting with Margaret and the president of Capitol Records, Gary Gersh, who was very

cool. He didn't want to force somebody to stay with him. He knew how great Elliott was, and did what he could to keep him, but he didn't want to do it over a gun.

Later on, Margaret, Elliott, and I met for lunch. The first 40 minutes of that meeting were *really* rough because he's so shy and doesn't say much. He had an orchestration book under his arm, and I actually pointed to it and said, "What do you have there?" That opened the conversation, and then it was a good solid hour of talking about music and some of the artists that I had been associated with that really affected him. He was saying, "I'm gonna start thinking about using an orchestra on my record." He was testing my response, I think. So I went into my Randy Newman and Van Dyke Parks speech about how interesting it is when you orchestrate and go beyond rock, and I think that pushed some of his concerns aside. I mentioned the right artists, and he relaxed.

MARGARET MITTLEMAN: It definitely started with Lenny. Elliott felt good knowing it was one of the top guys behind him, because it was a big, big jump.

LENNY WARONKER: He never felt intimidated musically, and he was quite open about things in the studio. We didn't stop by often, but when I was there, if I had a thought—even if it was bad—he would listen. It was almost like he was taking notes. I made some reference to The Beach Boys at one point, suggesting the possibility of adding an odd instrument, maybe a woodwind, and rather than either file it away or just go, "No," he was intrigued by it.

The harmonies and the vocal parts were so much more predominant on *XO*, and that gift, along with all the other gifts that he had, was a surprise. It shouldn't have been. You could tell from his earlier records that it was there, but not to that degree. He completely stepped up. I was so taken by what he was doing.

His stuff was always so precise. Most great songwriters are very economic, and he was, outside of Randy Newman ... well, I shouldn't say it this way. But he was as good as it gets when you're talking about layers within lyrics. There was so much in it with so few words, and as fragile as he sounded, he was in complete command.

ROB SCHNAPF: He was brisk in the studio. Speed was never the focus, but at the end of day one we had "Waltz #1" basically done. We came back the next day and added that big old bass drum to it, and added strings to it after that, but the meat of the song—vocals, everything—was done.

TONY LASH: There was a song on *XO* that was probably the best song we did, as Harum Scarum, back in 1989 or 1990. He reworked it for *XO*, and turned it into "Everybody Cares, Everybody Understands." The old song was called "Catholic." That was surprising to me. I think he ended up doing more of that later, pulling out really old ideas and reworking them.

Around this time, Smith contributes the original song "Miss Misery" to the Good Will Hunting *soundtrack. Soon after* XO *sessions are under way, they are interrupted by the news that the track has been nominated for an Oscar.*

GUS VAN SANT [*director,* Good Will Hunting]: I knew about Heatmiser, and I saw them one time at Pine Street [later changed to La Luna], which was the center of a lot of alternative bands during the '80s. But I didn't really know too much about their music. Mostly I had these two CDs from my friend Steve Birch, who worked for a lot of bands because he was an artist and designed covers. He'd picked up a bunch of CDs for me from this store called Locals Only around 1994, and *Roman Candle* was in the pile. Elliott's music was something I just happened to put on at one point. It reminded me of Simon & Garfunkel. Although, before I met Elliott, someone said, "Don't mention Simon & Garfunkel to him."

As I do with most films, I try and find some music that you could use throughout, not just a sampling of lots of different artists. And I thought it might be interesting to try that with Elliott. I told the editor, Pietro Scalia, who's now one of the most expensive editors in Hollywood, to try his music, and it just worked.

LARRY CRANE: I was out running errands or doing something, and I come back around and Elliott goes, "Oh, Gus Van Sant came over and I played him that song we recorded." And I'm just like, "What! I wasn't here?!"

The studio asked if we had anything original and unreleased we could put in there, and we played them "Miss Misery," and they thought it was great. Later, I was in the middle of a session, and I got this phone call like, "This guy's going to show up to grab the tape." They put a guy on a plane in L.A., and he flew up, and got in a limo—it wasn't just a goddamn cab, it was a *limo*—and pulled up in front of the studio later that same day. He grabs that one reel, jumps in the car, and goes back to the airport to fly back to L.A. What a joke.

Rob Schnapf and Tom [Rothrock] remixed the song down there, and then they basically had to pretend that it had been written for the movie in order to get an Oscar nomination. Elliott couldn't say it was actually tracked before he'd even heard of *Good Will Hunting*! It doesn't matter now, you know? [*laughs*]

SLIM MOON: *Either/Or* came out in February of '97, and *Good Will Hunting* came out later that year. But I had put out a lot of expensive records all in one year, and had kind of overdone it, and we were a small operation. I had gotten myself in a situation where I owed the manufacturer of the records a tremendous amount of money, and it was going to be four months before I started to see money trickling in from all of it. I had really screwed up.

So I was in my bedroom at the Las Vegas Hilton, of all places, at the National Association of Recording Merchandisers convention—I wasn't there just gambling away the money that I didn't have [*laughs*]—when Elliott's publisher called me and said he'd been nominated for an Oscar. That saved our business.

ROB SCHNAPF: I remember going into the studios and doing vocals and piano on "Miss Misery" pretty early in on *XO*, and all of a sudden he gets nominated for an Oscar and it just changes everything. It became really hard for him because, for one, he's playing everything, so he never has a break. Elliott plays drums, then plays bass, then plays guitar, then plays piano, then sings. And before that, he would have interviews from like 9 a.m. to 1 p.m. talking to people, international press, all over the place.

GUS VAN SANT: As soon as the nominations came out, all of us were assigned different campaign duties. Elliott played in a little club in TriBeCa near the Weinstein Company, which was partly organized by the movie promotion. It was just a simple thing, but it wasn't his own thing, so he was all nervous. He didn't really know what to wear, so he just put on some slacks. With his schedule, he didn't have a place to change, so he changed on the subway platform and got reprimanded by a cop.

MARGARET MITTLEMAN: We had to go to Capitol Studios and rehearse with the orchestra for the Oscar performance. They were impressed with his knowledge working with an orchestra and writing out his piece. We had a trailer, which was a trip to him. We saw the stage and what the audience was going to look like; there were all the signs on the chairs saying who was going to sit where.

They were trying to figure out how he would come out, how to make him perform. They wanted him to sit on the set of stairs that everyone would walk up to get to the podium, and we tried that. They really wanted him to be the guy who comes out and sits on the stairs. I walked out to [Oscars producer] Gil Cates, kind of shaking and saying, "I'm sorry, that can't happen. He's not going to do that." Elliott wouldn't say anything, so I had to do all that, which was very stressful.

LARRY CRANE: The Oscars people came to Margaret and said he's only going to be playing a verse and a chorus, and Elliott was like, "I don't want to do it then." Simple as that. So they said they'd just get someone else to play his song: "Here's Billy Joel!" Or it's Matt Damon in a top hat.

MARGARET MITTLEMAN: The day of the ceremony, me, Rob, Joanna, and Elliott pulled up to where all the limos were pulling up, and I was trying to figure out how to get Elliott down the red carpet, which was chaotic. The four of us started to walk down one side, but Rob and I got pulled away, like, "This is the side *you* go on." The photographers were just trying to figure Elliott out. Nobody knew who he was.

GUS VAN SANT: He had a white suit, and it was kind of amazing. As soon as the curtains parted, I saw that the entire stage was decorated as the Titanic. I thought, "Oh, I see." Hollywood was so excited that they had a movie that grossed a billion dollars and they were gonna show it. So Celine Dion had a full orchestra. Elliott had a little bit of an orchestra, too, but it was all very tiny in comparison. They used a lot of fog for the show, presumably because it was the Titanic, and it made me very sick—three hours of that stuff blowing on you and you just get a severe hangover.

ROB SCHNAPF: Celine Dion was really awesome to him. She really was.

"I would always watch his soundchecks, so I was sitting there, and he covered 'Thirteen' by Big Star. It just brought me to tears … His version of 'Thirteen' was devastating in that empty theater. I don't think he even knew I was there." —Lou Barlow

LARRY CRANE: I knew it had no chance in hell of winning. I was hoping it would, but come on; it's up against the song from *Titanic*. It's funny, the woman I'm married to now was my friend at the time, and she came and picked me up, and we went and watched the Oscars at La Luna. We had so much history with Elliott and Joanna there, and it was awesome because it was queer night at La Luna, so we went and watched it with all these wonderfully raging queens, who were like, "Oh, look, there she is, oh my god, she's beautiful!" whenever someone came onstage.

REBECCA GATES: If one of your friends is suddenly performing at the Oscars, there's a sense that something's shifted: a shift in opportunities, a shift in who's paying attention. I just loved that he was hanging out with Celine Dion. He was like, "Hey guys, you get so many weird gifts when you go the Oscars." He felt weird about it; it was a cool thing, but it was a weird thing. There's a part of being good friends where you try to keep things normalized. We just said, "You looked hilarious up on stage. You did a good job, it was excellent."

DORIEN GARRY: He had tremendously low self-esteem, so it was very awkward for him to all of a sudden be revered by so many strangers. Ultimately, I think that was the hardest and most confusing thing for him. He couldn't understand what the big deal was, I guess.

LUKE WOOD: He was extremely reluctant about promotion in general, but it wasn't because he thought he was too good for it, or because he thought it was selling out. It was really because he felt like the music should speak for itself, and everything else was redundant and irrelevant and silly. "Why do I talk about 'Waltz #2'? Listen to the song!" He really believed what the song meant to you is what it meant.

STEVEN DROZD: We ended up doing some shows in Sweden together with Elliott playing with his full band around '99. I was in pretty bad shape at that point, but we just really hit it off, and next thing I knew we were getting drunk and playing acoustic guitars on his tour bus, driving through Sweden. As miserable as I was on tour at that time—I was really strung out and I couldn't get anything in Scandinavia, and I was going two or three days without really sleeping—he and I would drink whiskey and play Elton John and Big Star songs at four o'clock in the morning on the tour bus. It was incredible.

FIGURE 8 (2000)

In 1999, as touring for XO *winds down, Smith begins working on what would eventually become its ambitious follow-up,* Figure 8.

AUTUMN DE WILDE [*photographer, cover art and inserts for* Figure 8; *director, "Son of Sam" video; author of the 2007 photo book* Elliott Smith]: We first met because I knew his manager, Margaret Mittleman. Later, we met on the street in New York and hung out that whole night. Someone had spray-painted "freak" in a bunch of places in New York, and he thought it was funny, so the next morning, I took some pictures of him standing in front of the word "freak." It was a very unofficial beginning. I was in no way pursuing work.

A bunch of time passed before Elliott's manager asked me to submit my portfolio, which was mostly photos of my friends, for *Figure 8*. I had a photo of Steve Malkmus from being on tour with them, and some photos of Beck, and probably the Eels. Then, at the back of that book was a photo of Elliott, and he realized whose portfolio he was looking at.

"He could play almost any instrument. He could go from bluegrass to folk. He would go, literally, from Chopin to picking up the guitar and playing a Minutemen riff. When you have someone that's that deeply gifted and special, you're really just lucky to be in the room."

—Luke Wood

One of my first questions was "Do you want to change anything about how you're portrayed?" He immediately said, "I feel like everybody thinks I just want to sit in little dark rooms and look depressed in my photos. There's never any color or light, but I love color so much." We talked about all the things he loved, like French New Wave. He was a cinephile, and he had great taste in movies.

I was warned by Margaret that he probably only wanted to do the photo shoot for a few hours, and that I should try to get as many photos as I could. But we shot for like 12 hours. People always said that he didn't like having his photo taken, but I think he didn't like the process as it had been presented to him up until that point. With us, it was a creative process, and he really enjoyed it. It wasn't just about 400 photos of Elliott Smith.

LUKE WOOD: Elliott was living in my neighborhood in Silver Lake at the time, and he demoed some of the *Figure 8* songs at my house because I had a small studio. He'd be there during the day while I was at work, and I would get to come home and hear these things as they came together and literally look at his sketchpads of lyrics. *Figure 8* is a *very* specific record. Just like *XO*, it's different lyrically and slightly more esoteric, but he had a real idea of what he wanted to say.

It was such a joy watching the thought he would put into small things as he wrote. Should it be "to" or should it be "at?" Should it be first person or second person? Should this be plural or singular? Where should I put the modifier? He would write five different versions of a sentence, only changing the modifier. His music was unbelievably well thought out.

AUTUMN DE WILDE: I went to a junior high down the street from the *Figure 8* wall—well, *now* it's the *Figure 8* wall; then it was the Sound Solutions wall. I have childhood memories of girls getting beat up in the parking lot of the McDonald's next to it. I took photos of a lot of murals and weird signs from Echo Park to Silver Lake and asked him, "What if this was our set?" He loved that idea because it was like seeing something he saw every day and didn't realize how amazing it was, which is a very Los Angeles thing. When you start narrowing your vision to one thing at a time, you start seeing little gems in the Los Angeles landscape.

ROB SCHNAPF: *Figure 8* was recorded all over the place, not all at once. *XO* got really hard to do because of him

playing everything, so for *Figure 8* I said, "When you have a batch of songs, let me go record them. We can do it in two-week spurts, that way it's not this huge, epic burden on you." There was one batch where he did it all, another batch where Sam [Coomes] was more involved playing bass. Then we were in England at Abbey Road, and [drummer] Joey Waronker happened to be in town with R.E.M. and we cut a bunch of songs [with him].

AUTUMN DE WILDE: He requested me to direct the "Son of Sam" video. I was shocked, and I think Dream-Works was pretty shocked, too. I hadn't directed a video before. To their credit, they rolled with it. It was inspired by *La Jetée* and *The Red Balloon*. I would never try to get rid of the sadness that was connected to his songs, but there is so much more in them—so much great poetry that represented abstract and direct ways of explaining how you feel to someone. Not everything was a diary. Some of it was role-playing, becoming other people and singing from their point of view.

TONY LASH: I didn't really dive into *Figure 8* very deeply. I could feel the emotional remove when I heard it, and I really didn't like that. *XO* still seemed more emotionally engaged. I remember telling him that I thought "Waltz #1" was my favorite song on *XO*, and he was like, "Yeah, that's the best one." That was a nice little re-bonding moment. Then the sound of *Figure 8* was like, "Here's a bunch of really good chord changes and notes." But it was missing that feeling of him directly engaging.

DORIEN GARRY: That was the period where things got unhealthy for him physically. He had someone on his crew who was a bad influence. Not someone in his band, but someone who was working for him, who was notorious for getting musicians drugs and doing them with them. I mean, I knew what a lot of that record was written about, and by that point everything felt so over the top and overwhelming that it was a little bit hard for me to just sit back and enjoy the music. Elliott definitely channeled whatever was wrong in his life or upsetting to him into his music like tenfold.

LOU BARLOW: I saw him at a party in L.A., and he was actually a really good croquet player. I learned croquet from Elliott. Anyway, I said something like, "I think I'm drinking too much." And he's like, "Well, can you feel your liver?" "What do you mean?" "When you drink too much, you can feel your liver literally pulsing from your side." I was poking for it, trying to feel it, and he's like, "Can you feel it?" And I'm like, "No! Where is it?" He's showing me where it is and telling me when it gets really bad, it pops out the side. I think it's something his dad had told him. I was like, "Man, I guess I'm really not that hardcore of a drinker—my liver isn't protruding from my chest."

ROB SCHNAPF: When he was on top of his game, none of that was happening. Did he drink? Yes. But when I go back and think about it, it started happening during *Figure 8*. It was not in the open. He was definitely not sharing it. But in retrospect, it explained some things.

JJ GONSON: He wasn't doing any drugs or really drinking very much when we were together. A big part of what tore us apart was talking about wanting to do drugs. I was like, "I just can't be around that." He didn't want me to tell him what not to do.

DORIEN GARRY: I maintained a friendship with him until he died. I mean, I live in Los Angeles now, and I'm not a fan of probably 75% of the people that call themselves Elliott's friends from L.A. I know the ones that are for real, who had healthy friendships with him. I'm always a little bit torn about speaking publicly about him—losing a friend like that is one of the most difficult things that's ever happened in my life. But if I don't do it, you know … the people who are eager and willing to talk are usually not the right people.

From the very beginning, we had a sibling relationship. I met him when I was 18, and you don't really understand a lot of things in the world when you're 18. Emotionally, he was the most vulnerable person I'd ever met at that point. We took care of each other during the not-so-fun times in our lives. I never cast judgment on him. I had to figure out a way to be concerned when there were moments to be concerned. There was a way to approach him about it, and a way not to. I think he appreciated the fact I was never going to do it the way he didn't want to hear it.

Elliott wasn't a typical alcoholic or drug addict in the sense that they try to keep it secret from people. He was very honest about what was going on. If there's one thing Elliott was not, it's a liar. It was hard. I don't know which is worse: being deceived or having it just be all out in the open like that. It was very, very upsetting to know that somebody I cared about so much was doing something so stupid.

MARGARET MITTLEMAN: As things got bigger, I probably talked to him less. My job had changed a little bit. I became a parent. I hired a friend who became my point person for Elliott. I would take the big-picture meetings with him, but as far as, like, "Can you deliver this list of interviews he doesn't want to do, please?" I stopped doing that. At the time, it was like "Okay, you stress me out, and I'm stressing you out. Let's have other people talk to each other and get our message across. I'll deliver it to her; she'll deliver it to you." That just became easier, and I didn't see anything wrong with that.

But somewhere in there, we lost him. I have my reasons and my thoughts of outside influences, where I feel like a parent, like, "Oh, if only they hadn't met that person." As if it were that person's fault. There were a couple of people who I wish we hadn't had in his circle at the time, in retrospect.

AUTUMN DE WILDE: His behavior was becoming more erratic. He's not the first person I've experienced this with, where drugs overtake the personality after a certain point. That's when you see that there is nobody who is enough of an individual to be an individual on drugs—even the most original person on earth, which I think he was. Some people hold onto their friends when they're sick like that, and some people systematically try to destroy their relationships in order to not drag them down with them. I don't know how much credit I should give him, but I felt like he systematically destroyed his relationship with anyone he really respected and cared about. Whatever was left of him did not want us around while he was totally down there.

MARGARET MITTLEMAN: We had tried once to have an intervention in Chicago [circa the *Either/Or* tour]. Oh my god. He hated us. He never let me forget what I did to him. We'd be having a great conversation, and it would just come up again out of nowhere. It totally reminds me of the child in him, or my own kids, how they hold on to one memory of mom and dad fighting at dinner. He never let me forget how betrayed he felt. He did agree to go. I think he felt the love and the concern, but you just don't do that to him. That's what he was like, "I'm a different person. You could have dealt with it differently."

"I'm always a little bit torn about speaking publicly about him—losing a friend like that is one of the most difficult things that's ever happened in my life. But if I don't do it, you know ... the people who are eager and willing to talk are usually not the right people." —Dorien Garry

Years later, when he started hanging out with Jon Brion wanting to do work with Jon and not Rob is where the lines *really* got blurred. This would have been around 2001. I just wanted what was best for my husband and for Elliott. By then, he was a different person. Honestly, he wasn't really nice to me. He came over one day during the Super Bowl—he used to spend every Super Bowl with us—and he looked like Pocahontas. He had long hair, in braids. I just didn't know him anymore. His girlfriend Valerie [Deerin] came over—that's another person who should have never been in his life—and he told Rob he wanted to work with Jon Brion.

That was heartbreaking. I didn't like the delivery. I didn't like his choice of day because that was something we'd done together. That was the beginning of the end for me. He came over fucked up with my kids in the house, and I just shut down. I just wanted to protect my husband and my family and myself. And when I quit, that pissed him off. That's the part that can make me cry. There was no closure. We never got to argue. We never got to hash it out. I was more like, "Just get out of here." I never was invited to his funeral. His drug abuse had turned him into something he wasn't when I knew him all these years.

ROB SCHNAPF: When it happened, he was all fucked up. I had already kind of told him I don't approve. "You want to smoke crack or whatever, that's your free will, great. I don't want to be around it. That's my decision."

DORIEN GARRY: At one point, I probably hadn't heard from him for about four or five months—he wasn't calling back, and it was pretty upsetting. The day after September 11, I came back into the house to an answering machine message from him. He didn't sound like himself—I mean, everybody sounded weird after Septem-

ber 11, but I knew that things were pretty dark for him at that point. But his message was asking if everyone was okay, talking about how he's taken the train and gotten off at the World Trade Center, how he'd done it over a million times. That meant a lot to me. But then I couldn't get a hold of him again for a long time. He was in a relationship that cut him off from a lot of people at the time. It was really terrible because I'd known him through some dark times already, but he always, always reached out.

SCOTT BOOKER [*manager, The Flaming Lips; briefly managed Smith*]: [The Flaming Lips] did a few dates in Europe with Elliott around '99, and we all got along really great. After that I got a call from him like, "Hey, would you be interested in being my manager?" I was like, "Of course, who wouldn't? You're a genius." I didn't really know what I was getting into. In our first conversation, he was like, "I want off DreamWorks."

He didn't want to record for them anymore because he was convinced that they had people following him, that they were breaking into his house. Those kinds of things. Which we all know wasn't true. But I'd be like, "Well, Elliott, I'm not gonna say I don't believe you, but why don't we get one of those cameras that you can buy for like five bucks, and you take pictures of any car or person that is following you." And he said, "Well, the cars have blank license plates." I never said, "I don't believe you." I tried to be pragmatic and realistic. He even said to me, "Well, it's probably not really there."

When The Flaming Lips played a show in L.A. one time, I remember him calling me saying, "DreamWorks are at my house because my Flaming Lips backstage pass was upside down on the floor." I was like, "Maybe you just dropped it." I was afraid to say those things, but I'd say it casually. And he was like, "No, I remember putting it on my desk." He'd have a very elaborate reason as to why. It just wasn't worth arguing with him.

Even though I didn't think his reasons were sound, I thought I should still let the label know he's uncomfortable being there and let them have a part of the decision as well. So I went and had a meeting with Lenny Waronker and Luke Wood. I said, "Look, I don't think this is a good idea for Elliott to not be on DreamWorks, and I know you guys love him, but for whatever reason, he's uncomfortable with this. What do you guys wanna do?"

Lenny came up with a pretty elegant solution. He was like, "Let's not say he's off the label. Let's just let him put this next record out wherever he wants to, as long as it's not another major label." I thought that was very fair of them, and I liked that they weren't going to just drop him. It solved the dilemma of that moment.

I mean, just think about me as the manager going into Lenny Waronker, this legendary, artist-friendly music-industry person I've looked up to my whole life, saying, "I don't think we should be on DreamWorks"—a label that any band would want to be on. It was just funny. But to some degree, maybe that's part of the reason why they agreed to it as well because they're artist friendly. They know that it was something bigger than an artist being mad at his record label.

LENNY WARONKER: I know Scott, and I don't remember that [meeting]. I do remember that Scott was gonna get involved, which I thought might be nice because I liked him. But I don't remember anything like that.

LUKE WOOD: Elliott was trying to find a place where he could be creative and happy. I think he felt somewhat restricted at a major label: having to do interviews, go on tour, have a commercial record. He didn't like that pressure. I deeply respected him as a musician and as a friend. He spent a lot of time at my house. He knew my baby. It was a really difficult period. There's a reason I haven't talked about it for 10 years.

FROM A BASEMENT ON THE HILL (2004)

In 2001, Smith begins and ends a series of recording sessions with Jon Brion, which fall apart after Brion confronts him about his drug use and self-destructive behavior. By the fall of that year, he contacts producer David McConnell.

DAVID MCCONNELL [*producer,* From a Basement on the Hill]: At the end of the *Figure 8* tour, he had just started recording with Jon Brion, but for whatever reason, he wasn't happy with that process, so he split ways with Jon and got in touch with me. When he called me he was actually in Big Bear, up in the mountains, and he was like, "Man, I want to start as soon as possible, can I come down tonight?"

I could tell he was really itching to get into the studio and work with a new producer, someone who was gonna do things a little more experimentally. He wanted somebody who wasn't so formulaic, who was willing to go down the path of discovery with him, and I guess he heard that maybe I would be that guy.

So I told him we should record in my private studio because that's where the more experimental equipment was. I told him he was welcome to stay in the house, too, because we had a guest room. The studio was beautiful. My ex-girlfriend actually owned the property, and it was almost like a compound, overlooking the Pacific Ocean. I had named it Satellite Park one day when I was walking around because it felt like I was on the moon or on an observatory somewhere.

When he showed up, it was around 2 a.m., and he was in two cars; his girlfriend [Valerie Deerin] was driving one car, and he was driving the other car, and both cars were full of all of his belongings. I mean *everything* from his apartment. I was thinking he was gonna show up with a suitcase and a backpack and a couple of guitars, but it was like five guitars, a giant keyboard, amps, and then five suitcases of clothes. He had toys, books, you name it. And then he had medication, and various other things.

He also brought all his two-inch reels that he was working on at Jon's house. So we drank a couple of beers, and I gave him the tour of the place and everything, and then he goes, "Okay, there's a song on here that I recorded by myself at Jon's place that I want to keep, that I really like. Why don't you just mix this song for me, and I'll be back in the morning." Then he left. He was like, "I've got some errands to run right now. I've got some stuff I gotta do." Remember, this is 2 a.m.—well no, by now it's 4 a.m., because we had talked about my philosophy on recording and producing for two hours.

So I put the reel on the machine and I started listening to the song, just by myself. And the first time I heard it, just pushing up the faders so I could hear the different instruments and his voice, I got the chills. It was one of the most haunting, beautiful songs I'd ever heard. It sounded nothing like the music I'd heard him do before. It sounded way more intricate, way more complex.

It reminded me of Rachmaninoff, but with lyrics, with a story. Sitting in there alone, I almost had an out-of-body experience because I knew that I was about to work on one of the best things I'd ever worked on in my life. So I spent the next three or four hours mixing the song, which was called "True Love is a Rose." It's a shame because that song never ended up on the album. He wanted it to be on the album, it was one of his favorites.

So he finally got back, listened to my mix, loved it, and then he says, "Let's start recording another song." At this point he probably hasn't slept in two days.

The next track we worked on was "Shooting Star." He told me he wanted it to have this psychedelic intensity, to take elements of Hendrix and The Stooges, but create something that couldn't be compared to anybody else. We slowed down the reel, just slightly, so it would have a euphoric, heavy, psychedelic persona.

"Shooting Star" has three drum sets: We would do one drum take, and then we would double the drums, and then sometimes triple them. If you listen closely on headphones, you'll hear the snare drums flailing because there are three kits going on. He and I talked about that. I'd say "Hey, you know, this sounds great, are you comfortable with having the snares slightly out of time?" And he was like, "Man, I love it." He wanted to embrace the human quality of this sound. That was very important for him.

He wanted "Shooting Star" to be the opening track then. "Coast to Coast," the opener on the album that got released, was another one we worked on together. He recorded the drum tracks at Sunset Sound studio with Steven [Drozd] from The Flaming Lips and the poet Nelson Gary's part at the end. He had two drummers playing live at the same time on that, he told me, and he stood in the middle of the room pointing at each drummer to do the changes, like he was doing his own version of conducting.

STEVEN DROZD: I went to Los Angeles to visit my then ex-girlfriend and now wife: We'd been broken up for a few years and she'd gotten into a serious relationship and then got out of the serious relationship, and I was trying to win her back. I contacted Elliott, and he said, "I know of this Suboxone doctor that's helped me greatly"—which is this drug you take to get off opiates—"and

I'm doing some recording. Could you come down and play some drums?" So we just set up the two drum kits and played at the same time. I know that you can be a highly functioning drug addict depending on what drugs you're getting into, but to me, it didn't seem like he was affected at all. He was fucking in charge of the session. People think I played drums all over that record, but it really just ended up being one song.

DAVID MCCONNELL: From that first night, he basically moved in and ended up living there with me for many months. And that's when we did the bulk of the album. We'd be in my bedroom, and he'd sit on the bed and play me songs really late at night. He played "King's Crossing" for me on his guitar one night, although that's not a song we worked on together.

He brought his guitars, but the funny thing about Elliott is he had five of the same guitar, the Gibson ES-330. I never understood it, exactly. I was like, "Okay, that's great, we can use those, but if you want this bigger guitar sound, I encourage you to check out the guitars that I have." On "Shooting Star," he fell in love with this old '60s Telecaster I have. Most of the really big guitars you hear on that album are that Telly because this guitar just spits at you.

He was constantly testing me. He always asked me what my favorite albums were, and it was important that they weren't ones that were super-produced, because his favorite records weren't slick; they weren't perfect. Elliott was very adamant not to use Pro Tools because he didn't want to fix things. That was one of the important things I learned from working with him on that record. The technically correct performance isn't beautiful. It's the performance that can't be replicated ever again.

One of the things that was really fun and worked well was, if we would double a guitar track, we would purposefully de-tune the guitar. So for the first track, we would make it a little bit sharp, and then for the second, we would make it a little bit flat. If you played one by itself it was kind of upsetting, but when they came together, all of a sudden you'd start smiling.

I'd never see anyone use drugs like Elliott before. I knew I couldn't give him an intervention because he'd already warned me. I knew that I couldn't say, "Hey, you have to leave," because if he wasn't with me, he'd end up somewhere else, which could potentially be harmful. I knew that at my place I could at least watch him.

"It's a cool, beautiful record. He wrote it when he was alive. He didn't write it when he was dead. He didn't write it after a suicide, or after a murder, or whatever the fuck happened. When he was writing it, he still wanted to live his life." —Rob Schnapf

I think I developed an anxiety disorder working with Elliott. He's one of the most complicated people I've ever known in my life. Every once in awhile we'd get in an argument, and he'd leave, and we wouldn't talk for a week. Then he'd call me and say, "This is stupid, let's go get a beer and talk." That was how the pattern went. The next day he'd be back at my place. But I loved him like a brother. I wasn't about to turn my back on him.

It got the point when he really needed his own place to finish the record, so I helped him put together his New Monkey Studio and then continued to work with him there. That went on for months and months, and then we kind of lost track. That was basically the last year of his life.

LOU BARLOW: I was seeing him more often around that period, too. He was talking about not doing as many drugs. He had been through a really bad period and the spark was kind of coming back. He was in this really bizarre period where he was dressing like Willie Nelson—he would wear these strange silk pants with embroidery down the side and long, flowing shirts. But then he started to look like Elliott again.

AUTUMN DE WILDE: As a photographer, I made a decision not to document that time period. That's not the kind of artist I am. I don't judge someone who does that at all, but that was not what I was there for. After that point, I was there as his friend until I wasn't welcomed as his friend. I know he loved me a lot, and I loved him a lot, but it's not the same person. Everybody who was a close friend basically had to say goodbye twice.

JJ GONSON: I talked to him on the phone around '99, and he was a mess. I hadn't spoken with him in a very long time because I had to say, "I can't be in touch with you anymore." The last thing he said to me was, "I'll write you a letter." Which of course he didn't do.

He burned every bridge that he crossed. He didn't just say, "Look, I need a break." He took a machete, chopped you into tiny little pieces, poured battery acid on it, then added salt and set you on fire. He did this painful, painful ripping-himself-away-from-people thing to protect himself. He genuinely believed, I think, that he was doing the right thing for other people. He had convinced himself that the world was better off not having him in it, for other people.

On October 21, 2003, Smith dies in an L.A. hospital at age 34 after suffering two stab wounds to the chest.

ROB SCHNAPF: He had been calling me the week before [his death] and was like, "Hey, I want to play you what I have for my record." I didn't call him back. I didn't know if I felt like dealing with it.

When our son was born in 1999, we got a phone call in the hospital room around midnight. It was Elliott. He was like, "Hey, would it be okay to come and hang out?" So he came down, and he was there all night. We wandered the hospital, just hanging out. It was really cool that he wanted to come share that special time with us. Sonny was born at eight in the morning; four years later, Elliott dies on [Sonny's] birthday. We were coming back from taking Sonny to see some big IMAX rocket ship thing, and I get a phone call from Luke Wood saying, "Hey, have you heard any rumors?" I was like, "No, why?" He said, "I just heard one that wasn't good."

MARGARET MITTLEMAN: I remember Sonny bopping around the backyard in his spacesuit. We were just having a family day. It was so bizarre because I had felt so removed. Somebody called Rob. I didn't get the call. That made me feel even worse.

ROB SCHNAPF: It was absolutely devastating. It's one of those things. You know one day your parents are going to die, and then they die, and it's still devastating, no matter how much you're prepared for it. A lot of people said, "Well, you must've not been surprised." But I was still fucking surprised.

AUTUMN DE WILDE: He died on my birthday, which has nothing to do with me except it happened to be my birthday. Then every birthday that follows, there's a period of mourning and a little sadness and I'm thinking, "Am I being really dramatic?" Part of what helps is imagining him laughing at me and just being like, "C'mon, dude. This isn't a movie about your life where the perfect, crazy dramatic ending is on your birthday."

STEVEN DROZD: We were in Seattle playing the last show of a tour opening for the Chili Peppers, and a very small percentage of the crowd cared about seeing us. We found out that night. It was just awful. I'm gonna start crying just thinking about it now. It was just so brutal. It fucked me up because I went to a bar in Seattle to try to escape, and then everyone in the bar is talking about it. People were visibly upset, crying. It was crazy.

DAVID MCCONNELL: I wasn't involved in the completion of [*From a Basement on the Hill*], which was interesting because Elliott and I had already mixed several songs for the album that were done. After his death, the family took over and brought in some really talented folks, but they hadn't been around for the process, so they didn't really know the plans he had for the record. I thought it was odd. I don't blame them, but I think they probably felt uncomfortable including me in the process because they equated me with that part of his life when he was using and not at his best. Maybe they thought that I was one of the bad guys. I really don't know. I can't speak for them. But it was unfortunate because there are many things that are different than what he wanted and planned for on that record.

Here's something I thought would have been groundbreaking: Two songs—"A Passing Feeling" and "Shooting Star"—were gonna be mixed in mono until a certain point where they'd break into stereo. We mixed those two songs that way, and there were moments when we cried listening to them. The impact was so profound. Anyway, the family never found those mixes for whatever reason. Also, the fact that it's missing two of the best songs is too bad. One of them is "True Love is a Rose" and the other one was called "True Friends / See You in Heaven." It's not that I'm bitter about that stuff, I just think the record would have been even more impactful. But I wasn't going to stick my nose in the family's business. They had just lost their son, and they were grieving. It wasn't my place to do that.

ROB SCHNAPF: Dave [McConnell] was kind of an asshole. I always tried to be really straight with him. Elliott stopped working with him—I don't know why—and he just felt like he knew exactly what Elliott wanted. Then he talked shit about me in the press without ever talking to me.

Elliott's sister [Ashley] had all the information, and she had been talking to Elliott a lot. She felt like she had a good understanding of where he was going. There was one song, "Abused," that the family didn't want on the album. Then there was another song called "Suicide Machines" that I thought was just asking for trouble if we included it. We just went through what was com-

pleted and worked off a sort of projected track order that Elliott had. There was stuff that wasn't finished, too. I don't even remember the names of the songs. I'd heard rumors about all this other material, but we never found it. I never heard it.

I had not worked on a friend's record who had died before. It was weird to hear him be very alive on those tracks. You would hear him go, "Let's do this." You'd hear him take a drag, inhale, blow out. You'd hear the piano stool creak, and you'd think, "He's alive." It was weird because, with all that stuff, you wouldn't normally think about it, like how you don't notice the hum of the refrigerator until the house is absolutely silent and it's three in the morning.

I was hoping for it to be a cathartic release, knowing at the same time it was never going to be how he planned it, because he wasn't there. All you could do was try. It was better than silence. It was positive and exciting on one hand, but the thing that bothered me was reading criticism about it that was unfounded. What were the options? Would you prefer to never hear the record?

People were saying of that album, "Oh, I like *this* version better, I liked the early versions better." *What?* There was nothing different. We didn't do anything. I didn't record anything. I took what was there and mixed it. So all those things that are unresolved are to be that way. Unresolved.

It's a cool, beautiful record. He wrote it when he was alive. He didn't write it when he was dead. He didn't write it after a suicide, or after a murder, or whatever the fuck happened. When he was writing it, he still wanted to live his life.

DORIEN GARRY: There was a space and a time after he died when I almost forced myself to listen to him a lot at home, alone, trying to process. It was a little bit cathartic. But now it's the opposite. I can't even listen to it. I've been at a coffee shop a couple of times when it's come on, and it's a hard few minutes to get through. I hope that changes. I trust that it will. I think I'll go through another wave of grief where I can listen to him and not feel like I miss him.

ROB SCHNAPF: There was a lot of crassness and a lot of disappointing behavior from people who were supposedly his friends. But the interesting thing is this is how history is written. The ones who were there aren't always

"The technically correct performance isn't beautiful. It's the performance that can't be replicated ever again."

—David McConnell

the ones who speak. But if people are going to go back and use this as a reference, then it should be truthful.

He would have had a great career. He would be on his own right now. He'd be like Wilco. He'd be able to do whatever he wants. He wouldn't need the business. He wouldn't need it at all.

I don't really listen to the records. Elliott still makes me sad, to be perfectly honest. I enjoy it in little bits, but I end up in this particular place, so.

JJ GONSON: When I decided I needed to shut off, I really shut him off. I never heard *From the Bottom of the Hill,* whatever it's called. I don't know his new songs. I really don't even listen to the old stuff.

AUTUMN DE WILDE: A bunch of us were tricked by journalists at the beginning, that's why everyone's pretty prickly about it. That was like an incredible breach of trust, and there was a great silence for a long time, from all of us.

But the loss of any friend takes a long time to heal. And then when you're sharing that friend with people who didn't know him—which is totally fine and amazing because I would like everyone to know who he was, and I wish they could have sat with him—it's even weirder. When you tell people that you feel really sad about your grandma dying, they go, "Oh shit, I'm sorry." But when it's someone famous, often you don't say it because immediately you worry: Does it seem like I'm name-dropping? So on top of trying to heal from losing a friend, you're trying to manage all the bullshit in your head: What are my reasons for bringing this up right now? Is it to say that I knew him? Am I now that person crying in public so that they can say they knew him? Like, what the fuck?

LUKE WOOD: I have not spoken about Elliott since his death. I spoke to many people the week he passed, but that was about trying to express how gifted he was, trying to articulate my thoughts of him as an artist. I

thought it was so important that what people remembered about Elliott was his work and not his death. My catharsis was on my own time.

NEW MOON (2007)

In 2007, Kill Rock Stars releases the rarities and B-sides compilation New Moon; *overseen by Larry Crane, the album features liner notes by, among others, Sean Croghan and Rebecca Gates.*

LARRY CRANE: Initially, *New Moon* was going to be a bonus version of *Either/Or,* like an extra disc from that same era. But they decided that that was not necessary. I called [Elliott's father] Gary, and we talked about the latest idea, which was a larger, more comprehensive B-sides and rarities compilation. We discussed what it involved, and I wrote up a little proposal of how much it would cost, what I was going to do. I knew I had to go to L.A. and dig through the vaults where the tapes were stored and do some research. This really opened up the question of, "Shouldn't somebody archive this? We don't know what's on any of these reels until you hear them." And he said, "Would you like to do it?" I didn't expect that to be his response, but I thought, "Well gosh, I guess I could do that."

Luckily, I was able to contact Rob Schnapf, Tony Lash, Neil Gust, even Jon Brion, and all these different people and ask questions, which made a big difference. Initially, it was *New Moon* and then the archive job, but I wish I could have done it in the opposite order—I wish I could have done as much archiving as I could do, and then pull *New Moon* out of what I found. It wouldn't be that different, but we have better tape transfers now. It would have sounded a little better. And maybe there were a few more songs that could've made it. But that's okay. It's a good record.

AUTUMN DE WILDE: My relationship with that *Figure 8* wall now is conflicted. Not because I have any grievanc-

es about it, but it was my wall that nobody cared about, you know? But I'm so glad because I love the Serge Gainsbourg wall—I don't have any painful memories attached to the Serge Gainsbourg wall. So I tend to not get too close or read anything on it. It's so awesome that people are repainting it, but it's burned in my head—this mural from childhood—so I can't help but think that they painted it wrong. I don't mean to sound like an asshole. I just mean they didn't reproduce it exactly the same, so for me it's like a weird blip, an awkward thing to look at because my eyes are trying to correct it.

LUKE WOOD: I've been fortunate to work with a lot of great artists in my career, but as a composer and a per-

former, Elliott was profoundly unique. The way he used harmonic structures. He could sit down to the piano and play Rachmaninoff. He could play almost any instrument. He could go from bluegrass to folk. He would go, literally, from Chopin to picking up the guitar and playing a Minutemen riff. When you have someone that's that deeply gifted and special, you're really just lucky to be in the room.

SCOTT BOOKER: I always said *Either/Or* is one of my top 10 albums of all time. The sad thing is I can't listen to it anymore. It's too hard. I'll put it on and my mind just starts thinking of things that I don't want to think about while listening to a record I love.

TONY LASH: For better or worse, there's a certain amount of locking Elliott away as I knew him. There are obviously a lot of reasons to be sad about him passing, but one of the things that I found most sad was that there was a lot of deterioration that happened. For the most part, people always have the capacity to change for the better. He had become distant from my life, and our relationship had fallen by the wayside, but I always felt like he was probably the single most talented musician that I ever worked with. Once we repaired our friendship, I thought there was always the potential we could do something again some day. When he died, that possibility was taken away, along with the possibility that he could find those really wonderful parts about himself again.

JJ GONSON: I didn't talk to anybody for like eight years. I couldn't do it. I just couldn't deal. The edge needed to wear off a little bit, because it was so raw. Elliott and I have mutual friends who talked a lot, right at the beginning. Now they're like, "I'm done, I never want to hear his name again." It's interesting. Recently, it's been kind of nice: People want to know, and I appreciate that as a music lover. Elliott was fantastic. He was a hilariously funny, super-fun person to be with, someone I absolutely adored with every microfiber of my body. It will always be a hard process, but I do feel some reconciliation in other people coming together. ✐

The Lighter Side of Elliott Smith

SLIM MOON: There was one show in a sports bar in Santa Cruz with no one there except the regulars, who were really bummed that we were bogarting their dartboard area. And I had really bad gas—I was farting up a storm. Elliott was cracking jokes about the smell between songs, to the amusement of no one but me.

DORIEN GARRY: He's been turned into somewhat of an icon, but he was actually a total goofball most of the time. He would prank call me and leave me voicemails. This was before cell phones, so I'd come home and there'd be a message that was him basically doing a whole Jerky Boys skit on the answering machine.

DORIEN GARRY: He had a real thing about clowns—being fascinated and intrigued by clowns, trying not to be scared of clowns. It was a constant joke. Clowns are weird. Clowns are cool. Clowns are rad. When I saw that story recently about the scary clown in Northampton who's been terrorizing people, the first thing I thought was, "Man, I wish Elliott was here for this."

LARRY CRANE: One day, he must have seen someone wearing a Big Dog sweatshirt—that brand—and he must have thought it was really funny because for no reason, he kept going around the studio puffing his chest out and repeating, "I'm a big dog." He wouldn't stop until it cracked us up.

REBECCA GATES: We were a pretty silly crew on tour. One time I was sitting shotgun in the van with my head in a book, and I heard this snickering behind me. I turned around and [Elliott] had taken electric tape and made an Abe Lincoln beard on his face. And every time I kept turning around, more people had this electric tape facial hair.

AUTUMN DE WILDE: For Elliott and I, the best part of the ["Son of Sam"] video was how funny it was trying to get this balloon to behave. If it was windy we were fucked, you know? I later found out that *The Red Balloon* had this giant puppeteering crane. Luckily, we did a test day. Somewhere, there is a clip of Elliott slapping his arms in dismay and being overwhelmed by the balloon hitting him in the face for like the 70th time. It was on one of those giant stairways in Echo Park that I think was in a Laurel and Hardy film, and he's at the top. He was just looking really pissed off, like he was gonna get in a fight with the balloon, and then laughing, and then angry again. The art director figured out you had to use fishing poles, and you can see it in one shot. At the end of the video, when the balloon dies, we all got really sad—and then we were laughing hysterically at how attached we had gotten to this badly behaved actor.

LOU BARLOW: He was accumulating so much gear at that time, too. He was on eBay constantly, managing a slew of auctions. This was for his studio, New Monkey, that he was building in North Hollywood. This guy who was playing drums in The Folk Implosion was also scheming heavily to be in Elliott's band and hanging around Elliott constantly. Every time he'd hang out with him, he'd come back with a different piece of equipment, like, "Yeah, Elliott handed this to me." "What? That's a $750 contraption for Christ's sake!" All of this stuff of Elliott's started accumulating in my practice space. "Wow! Where did you get that bass?" "Oh, Elliott gave it to me last night." "Really? That's a $2,000 bass." He would just be really high and tell the guy, "Yeah, you should take it."

STEVEN DROZD: He and I did ecstasy on the tour bus one night, and we were listening to Elton John's *Greatest Hits*. His favorite was actually "Goodbye Yellow Brick Road," so we played that one a lot. My favorite Elton John song is "Daniel." My son is named Daniel, and he's partly named after my wife's father, but also partly named after that song. So we get to that song, and Elliott stops it, and I'm like, "Hey, what are you doing?" He says, "Man, I never liked that fuckin' song. Who is this fuckin' Daniel guy, anyway." I try to tell him it's this character whose brother had been to Vietnam, and how they cut out the last verse because it was too weird, trying to sell him. He wasn't having any of it. "I don't give a shit! Fuck 'Daniel.' We're skipping 'Daniel.'"

Afterword

Many of us have a loved one who has died in tragic or shocking circumstances. Few of us, however, are unlucky enough to share that person with strangers. I had this thought over and over as I contacted the weary, defensive, resigned, ambivalent, and always gracious associates and friends of Elliott Smith for "Keep the Things You Forgot." Many of these people—managers, bandmates, girlfriends, producers—were having this conversation for the 15th or 20th time. Once again, a reporter interrupted their lunch hour or their Sunday afternoon to ask them about someone they loved who remained dead.

As I went about assembling this oral history, I was aware of my place in a fraught lineage. Reporting on Elliott Smith since his death has largely been a thankless task, leaving only bitterness in its wake. My goal was to tell an honest story about Elliott that would make everyone involved feel (mostly) good about having participated. I was (mostly) successful: The angriest note I received from a participant was more of a minor yelp of protest. People were less contented with their quotes about the end of his life, but this is understandable: What honest thing could we say about a friend in low times that we'd be happy seeing in print?

Nonetheless, the stories here are from people who felt they *had* to contribute, whether they wanted to or not. As Rob Schnapf told me, "This is how history is written. The ones who were there aren't always the ones who speak." Another contributor, calling me back for the third time to agonizingly clarify an offhand remark, apologized: "You have to understand. With all of this, it's because we still have his voice in our heads." Several interviewees told me this was the last time they ever planned to "do this" —go back to this place, revisit these complicated memories.

For this version in *The Pitchfork Review*, I reached out to some of the people who declined to be interviewed in the first round, for one reason or another, to see if they felt like commenting now. They remained resolute. There are stories left to be told, in other words, about Elliott, from major players in his life. But maybe those stories belong with those who knew him. The stories here, then, can be treated much like his music: A finite resource, but one to be cherished forever.

—*Jayson Greene, 2014*

Jayson Greene *is managing editor at eMusic and a columnist at* Pitchfork. *His writing has appeared in* BuzzFeed, Village Voice, GQ.com, XXL, MySpace, *and* NewMusicBox. *He lives in Brooklyn.*

The #Art of the Hashtag

Lindsay Zoladz

Thanks to Twitter, the hashtag has become an important linguistic shortcut. But while everyone from Robin Thicke to Beyoncé has used the symbol as part of their art, only a few have truly taken advantage of its culture-jamming possibilities.

Time moves quickly on the internet, so we are already overdue for a moratorium—and a subsequent nostalgic reflection—on something that happened a year ago. You might remember the summer of 2013 as the summer of hashtags in song titles or, more likely, the summer of internet think pieces about hashtags in song titles. In hindsight, the timing makes sense. Crowning a Song of the Summer is a fun but shameless pageant, and the list of hashtag hopefuls reads like a parade of contenders waving the flags of their own built-in PR campaigns: Mariah Carey and Miguel's "#Beautiful," Jennifer Lopez and Pitbull's video for "#LiveItUp," Miley Cyrus' "#GETITRIGHT," and Busta Rhymes' "#Twerkit," to name a few. The ever technologically overzealous will.i.am doubled down, releasing a single with Justin Bieber called "#thatPOWER," off his record *#willpower*.

The hashtag as we know it dates back to July 2009, and early uses of the symbol centered on uniting niche communities and political organizing, like the Arab Spring protests. In short order, advertisers and network broadcasters caught on

and began placing omnipresent hashtag "bugs" in the bottom of TV screens. Musicians are some of the most popular Twitter users, and tweets have been influencing rappers' cadences for years (Kanye West, Drake, and Big Sean have each claimed to have invented "hashtag rap," while some argue that the flow is as old as rap itself), so it's almost surprising that it took until last year for actual hashtags in song titles to trend.

I do not think we will ever see a summer like the #SummerOf2013 again because this experiment didn't exactly work—none of these songs became huge hits. (Ironically, the eventual song of the summer, Robin Thicke's "Blurred Lines," knowingly parodied hashtag mania in its video.) There were early warnings that hashtag song titles lead only to annoyance and confusion. Take synth-pop act Cobra Starship's 2011 single "#1Nite"—while the song's trend-friendly title was ahead of its time, a hashtag preceding a number wasn't the smartest idea, and many perplexed fans and radio DJs took to calling the song "Number One Night."

Many of the 2013 hashtag songs lead to similar

dissonance, probably because their would-be trending topics were too vague and too common. When you search #willpower, you do not see throngs of fans tweeting their love of will.i.am's latest album, but instead see people evangelizing the virtues of e-cigarettes and complaining about how hard it is to give up sweets for Lent. The "#LiveItUp" stream is awash with Twitpics of mani-pedis and YOLO-esque musings on the transience of youth ("high school will be done before you know it so #liveitup"). Quite predictably, the star of a "#Twerkit" search is not Busta Rhymes. These songs have now outlived their trending moments (if they ever had them to begin with), which makes something about the hashtags affixed to their titles feel desperate and sad. They have an air of Gretchen Wieners, forever trying to make "fetch" happen.

The oddest and perhaps most tragic case is "#Beautiful," the best song in the bunch. Most of these other #2013 songs sound cloyingly of the moment, but Mariah and Miguel's breezy Motown homage feels timeless—it's the kind of song that a wedding DJ could easily segue into "Build Me Up Buttercup" or "My Girl." Twenty years from now, it'll sound every bit as great as it sounds this afternoon, but thanks to its bad tattoo of a title, "#Beautiful" is forever doomed to show its age.

If you have any doubt that the hashtag is a frighteningly powerful tool in our modern vocabulary, imagine a person you care about texting you that song's title line out of the blue: "You're beautiful." Now think of the same person texting, "You're #beautiful." The second one is jokey, ironic, distant—and hey, maybe that's what that person was going for. But it also hammers home a point that the internet too often asserts: You're not as original as you once thought. "Beautiful" is analog, unquantifiable, one in a million. #Beautiful, on the other hand, is crowded terrain. Ten more people have just tweeted about something

or someone #beautiful since you started reading this sentence.

And yet, I feel compelled to defend the hashtag, if only for the selfish reason that I've noticed it creeping into my thoughts, my speech, and my non-Twitter vocabulary, and I want to believe I'm not crazy. (Or the punch line of a Jimmy Fallon skit.) Seems like I'm not alone, at least. "The hashtag," D. T. Max wrote in a recent *New Yorker* profile of Twitter founder Jack Dorsey, "has become so popular that people often insert jokey ones into their emails." Guilty as charged. My text messages to friends are now dotted with goofy, unclickable hashtags, and right before I sat down to write this, I dashed off an email to a friend with a link to something we'd been talking about earlier, with the subject line: "#relevant." Why not just "Relevant"? Well, for one thing, "#relevant" feels more casual, more intimate, more knowingly ironic—like you're shrugging off any claim to profundity. You're aware that you're not one in a million; you're in on that cosmic joke.

A common complaint used to be that there was no way to express sarcasm on the internet. Half a million people belong to a Facebook group called We Need A Sarcasm Font, and I'm sure a much larger number than that has experienced some kind of fight, misunderstanding, or needless worry over something someone said to them online that they read the wrong way. We're working on it, though.

As more and more of our daily interactions become text-based—people preferring texts to phone calls, workplaces that rely heavily on email and instant messaging—we're developing ways to stretch our written language so it can communicate more nuance, so we can tell people what we mean without accidentally leading them on or pissing them off. Periods have become more forceful, commas less essential, and over the last few years, the hashtag has morphed into something resembling the fabled sarcasm font—the official key-

Lindsay Zoladz *is an associate editor at* Pitchfork, *where she writes* Ordinary Machines. *Her writing has also appeared in* The Believer, Slate, Salon, Bitch, *and more. She lives in Brooklyn.*

stroke of irony. Putting a hashtag in front of something you text, email, or IM is a sly way of saying "I'm joking," or maybe more accurately, "I mean this and I don't at the same time." This is why the comedically oversized "#THICKE" that fills the screen in the "Blurred Lines" video

of being sold to. As far as culture jamming goes, its revolutionary potential is admittedly mild—the less risky and legal equivalent of graffiting a subway ad. But it's heartening to see that pretty much any major ad campaign's hashtag gets hijacked by people complaining

> Twenty years from now, it'll sound every bit as great as it sounds this afternoon, but thanks to its bad tattoo of a title, "#Beautiful" is forever doomed to show its age.

speaks the language of the hashtag better than the comparatively earnest *#willpower* or "#LiveItUp." #THICKE knows its own absurdity, and it knows that you know its absurdity, but on some level it would still very much like you to tweet about Robin Thicke.

about how dumb that ad campaign is. My personal recent favorite was KFC's #IAteTheBones, a slogan for boneless chicken wings that quickly devolved—or evolved—into a stream of sexual innuendo and jokes about cannibalism. The latest instance of this is Sprint's campaign

> **A list of things that, much to will.i.am's probable chagrin, are mentioned on the #willpower Twitter stream, as much or more than will.i.am.:**
> *Girl Scout Cookies, Ribs,* Candy Crush, Flappy Bird, *Cigarette, CrossFit, The Paleo Diet, Juice cleanses, Chocolate, Cake, Managing to bake a chocolate cake without licking the spoon even once*

Irony gets a bad rap thanks to ugly mustaches and unfunny T-shirts, but it can actually be liberating—a playful freedom from the straitjacket of always meaning exactly what you say. It can also be an expression of dissent. As quickly as companies realized that they could use the hashtag as an advertising tool, Twitter users realized that they could use sponsored hashtags as a way to talk back to the whole idea

for their new "friends and family plan" which peddles the hashtag #framily; most of the tweets in the #framily feed make fun of the ad executives who are desperately trying to make "#framily" happen.

Hashtags open up the potential of allowing the consumer to influence the ad campaign—or the TV show, or the song. But it's also worth asking if this is necessarily a good thing. Since the great failure of the #SongOfTheSummer2013, the next experiment might be to make songs out of hashtags that are already popular, in an attempt to make sure-fire hits from focus-grouped sentiments. Will this year's hopefuls be more like R&B singer Rico Love's "Bitches Be Like" (inspired by the popular #BitchesBeLike hashtag), or Pharrell's new duet with Miley Cyrus "Come and Get It Bae" (a wink to a favorite online term of endearment)? On the internet, we tend to talk about "connection" as something unequivocally positive, but constant connection can also stifle creativity and originality by making artists too self-aware, too concerned with metrics, too eager to please.

If there's a sweet spot between being obliviously disconnected and desperately hashtag-crazed, nothing has hit it with more precision than *Beyoncé*. In a world of SoundCloud mixes and Bandcamp pages, the surprise album is more like a sponsored Tumblr post—a sleek, unabashedly expensive-sounding record that speaks the internet's language without ever pandering for likes. The Chimamanda Ngozi Adichie TED Talk in the middle of "***Flawless," for instance, appears with sudden and delightful incongruence, like an artful photo Tumblr reblogging a dense block quote.

I will admit that something about "***Flawless" bothered me the first few times I heard it. Coming right after Adichie's critique of the different social expectations we hold for women and men, the quotable refrain "Ladies, tell 'em, 'I woke up like this'" struck me as a mixed message. It felt unwittingly conservative, the way that the "Single Ladies" chorus ("If you liked it then you shoulda put a ring on it") paid lip service to empowering single women but in the end just felt like an endorsement of eventually "putting a ring on it." The Beyoncé we see even in her most "candid" moments (or the song's comparatively unpolished video) definitely *did not* wake up like this. For Beyoncé to deny the effort it takes to look like Beyoncé seems like another way of keeping those unrealistic expectations about femininity in place. How can you quote a speech about the social, political, and economic equality of the sexes one

moment, and then shrug off the invisible but very real labor that goes into looking hot?

My initial read of the song, though, was too literal. As #wokeuplikethis has become one of the record's most popular memes, I've come to appreciate the phrase's irony and complexity. (The exaggerated, imminently GIF-able way she delivers the line in the video gives a hint she doesn't want us to take this statement too sincerely.) #wokeuplikethis is a perfect instance of "I mean this and I don't at the same time"—a way to both point toward the tyrannical digital-era expectation that women should always be camera ready, while at the same time celebrating the art of looking (and feeling) so goddamn *fine*. These are not contradictions, but the complexities of a feminism that comes from lived experience rather than hollow, you're-with-us-or-you're-against-us sloganeering. *Beyoncé*'s perspective reminds me of how writer Joan Morgan calls for "a feminism brave enough to fuck with the grays" in her 1997 hip-hop feminist manifesto *When Chickenheads Come Home to Roost*.

The ubiquitous hashtags that *Beyoncé* has spawned—#surfbort, #flawless, #wokeuplikethis—now feel inevitable, but they weren't screaming "tweet me!" in our faces the way "#LiveItUp" and #willpower were. We had to dig them out, so in a way, we completed them. The #wokeuplikethis meme feels like a genuinely collaborative effort—an example of how a hashtag can enrich a song's meaning rather than cheapen it. *Beyoncé* reminds me of something else Morgan says in *Chickenheads*, which was written more than a decade before the hashtag but somehow captures its slippery, collaborative spirit. "Trying to capture the voice of all that is young black female was impossible," she writes. "My goal, instead, was to tell my truth as best I could from my vantage point on the spectrum. And then get you to talk about it. This book by its lonesome won't give you the truth. Truth is what happens when your cumulative voices fill in the breaks, provide the remixes, and rework the chorus." ✐

Blind Date: Odd Squad's *Fadanuf Fa Erybody*

Jeff Weiss

A B-boy stoner met a blind wunderkind at a talent show in 1989. Five years later, Devin the Dude, Rob Quest, and Jugg Mugg released the overlooked rap classic *Fadanuf Fa Erybody*. Jeff Weiss recounts the Houston group's unlikely story.

All successful talent shows are alike, but each unsuccessful talent show is unsuccessful in its own way. The one held at Texas Southern University circa 1989 was a uniquely victorious failure. Its ashtray spawned Houston's Odd Squad: Devin the Dude, Rob Quest, and Jugg Mugg. The raunchy stoners' only record, 1994's *Fadanuf Fa Erybody,* was famously named Rap-A-Lot's best release by Scarface. But first came the talent show fiasco.

For weeks, fliers touted Kurtis Blow as the celebrity judge. The winner was promised $500 and a contract to record a 12-inch. But by show time, the Bronx legend behind "The Breaks" had gone AWOL, and the college auditorium was completely empty, save for the participants and a few family members. The show's director shambled aimlessly, biding time for Blow.

Raised in St. Petersburg, Florida, Devin the Dude split his adolescence between Houston and railroad country, East Texas. After high school, he moved back to H-Town in search of a record deal and a '79 Seville. At this point, Devin's dude archetype is as iconic in pot culture lore as Jeff Bridges. His solo catalog and hook on Dr. Dre's "Fuck You" give him Rap Hall of Fame credentials. But in the latter half of the '80s, he was Devin the Fat Square Twista, a B-boy known for popping, ticking, and gliding like an extra from *Breakin' 2: Electric Boogaloo*, and the talent show seemed like a legit chance in a city then lacking an established hip-hop infrastructure. So the excited teen made a stop-and-pause cassette tape of Roger Troutman instrumentals to rap over. But as soon as he graced the stage, the heckling began.

"There I am with my beat tape and my furry Kangol, and someone in the audience says, 'Who do you think you are, Slick Rick?'" recalls Devin, wheezing his molasses laugh. He has the most photographic memory of anyone you'll ever meet. He remembers gear details, dialogue, and the performance order from a talent show that occurred a quarter century ago, making him a one-man scientific study refuting claims that weed impairs your memory. (He also does impressions with pitch-perfect cartoon mimicry.)

"So I rap: 'It's not Slick Rick, it's this big dick Slim ... ' and start dissing him back," Devin says, rapping the old bars. "He gets upset and keeps talking shit. It was the longest three and a half minutes of my life." The judges weren't impressed. The day would've been completely worthless were it not for Quest's performance.

"I want to get everyone's attention, right quick," the administrator called out to the yawning crowd before Quest got onstage. "Do you think it's fair to let this guy participate in the talent show today?" He pointed at a hazel-eyed 17-year-old clutching his mother's shoulder. It was Quest, afflicted by sarcoidosis, an inflammation of the liver, kidney, and spleen. The disease had caused slow blindness since his diagnosis at age 12.

"[Quest] didn't look blind at all, so we were like, 'Why *shouldn't* he be allowed to perform? What's going on here?'" remembers Devin. "No one had a problem, of course—no one even knew what he was talking about."

"So his mom let him go. He plugged in that beat machine, twiddled with the buttons, pressed start on that motherfucker, and nearly blew the speakers out," the Dude continues. "It was some hard N.W.A or Public Enemy-type shit. He sounded like a mini-Ice Cube. I'm like, 'What in the *fuck*?' Everybody was tripping. And in my mind I'm thinking, 'Yessir, I agree, he *shouldn't* be allowed to compete in this talent show.'"

Quest's mom had forced him to sign up. Unable to play basketball or video games, music became a serious hobby shortly after the onset of blindness. Before meeting Devin Copeland, though, Quest

never considered doing it professionally.

"Out of that whole roomful of MCs, Devin was the only one who talked to me," says Quest, born Robert McQueen. Quest is at home in Houston, his voice several octaves deeper than his rapid-fire whistle of '94. The producer/rapper is in good health lately, after cirrhosis caused him to receive a liver transplant in 2011. "[Devin] wanted a beat and asked if I wanted to get a beer," Quest adds. "I told him that I lived right around the corner, and he was like, 'Cool, I got a joint too.' I told him, 'I don't fuck with any of that shit, but let's go.' The rest was history."

This plotline mirrors a Reagan-era after-school special: The cool break-dancing rapper in a Kangol (played by Doug E. Doug) befriends an insecure blind producer at a local talent show (a young Jamie Foxx). They both lose, but derive strength by bonding through the power of music. The reality was more R-rated, somewhere between *Up in Smoke, The Weird World of Blowfly,* and *Dancer in the Dark*. "Until then, I was losing my sight and not going out much," says Quest. "Devin was the first cat to embrace me and adopt me like a brother, teaching me how to dress and fuck with hoes."

But the Odd Squad didn't form that first afternoon. It took Devin a year to convince his partner Jugg Mugg to see the light. "Devin called me up the first day he met Rob and tried to get me to come over, but I was like, 'A blind producer? Get the fuck outta here,'" says Jugg Mugg (government name: Dexter Johnson), who had been in various groups with Devin, including a break-dance crew called 3-D and the more politically minded KKK (Krazy Kush Kings). "But after I didn't go, he told me again," he continues. "If you know Devin, you listen if he tells you something twice. It rarely happens."

Jeff Weiss *is a writer based in Los Angeles. He edits* Passion of the Weiss, *co-hosts the Shots Fired podcast, and is the co-author of* 2Pac vs. Biggie: An Illustrated History of Rap's Greatest Battle.

"I'm like, 'What in the *fuck*?' Everybody was tripping. And in my mind I'm thinking, 'Yessir, I agree, he *shouldn't* be allowed to compete in this talent show.'"—DEVIN THE DUDE

Quest's home studio became an unofficial hub of the Houston rap scene. Initially cutting records to cassette, the group quickly graduated to a four-track. With Devin's encouragement, the visually impaired producer seamlessly absorbed the arts of inhaling and rhyming. On any given day, UGK, Big Mello, Big Mike, Ganksta N-I-P, and DJ Screw popped up at Odd Squad headquarters to torch Swishers of skunk, drain 40s of Country Club, and freestyle.

It became Quest's turn to take the initiative. After several years of crate digging, producing, engineering, and home recording, he told his Odd Squad partners that it was time to step it up. They got a bio written, took press pictures, and finagled their way into a local art institute's studio to cut their demo. DJ Screw scratched and cut on the record, an artifact since lost to the Bermuda Triangle of the Rap-A-Lot archives.

Like the Odd Squad, Screw's early sound genuflected to the East Coast Catholicism of Run-D.M.C., Marley Marl, and Pete Rock. But the Odd Squad's lyrics and harmonies were closer to Southern Baptists gone to sin. The trio behind "Your Pussy's Like Dope" and "Smokin' Dat Weed" grew up singing in the church choir. Devin was conscripted to croon after repeatedly falling asleep during services. His punishment ended up being the group's gain, with his filthy, wobbly hooks doubling as narcotic hymnals. "We'd smoke on some Indian tribal shit and start humming old slave spirituals," Quest says, describing the genesis of the melodies. "We'd do chants for 10 minutes straight … almost like a trance."

There's nothing remotely surprising about rappers singing in 2014, but when *Fadanuf Fa Erybody* dropped in February of 1994, it was a fairly radical concept (lest you be deemed soft like P.M. Dawn). Prior to the Odd Squad, Rap-A-Lot built their reputation on body-in-the-trunk gangsta rap. Geffen had refused to distribute the Geto Boys, deeming their lyrics "violent, sexist, racist, and indecent."

Rap-A-Lot's most famous album cover pictured Bushwick Bill, bloody bandage hanging from his shot-out eye, getting carted from the hospital by Willie D and Scarface. By contrast, *Fadanuf*'s cover riffed on Ernie Barnes' "Sugar Shack," complete with psychedelic animations of Devin, Rob, and Jugg getting fucked up and freaking fleshy, bow-legged girls. Rap-A-Lot signing the Odd Squad was like if Death Row released *Bizarre Ride II the Pharcyde*.

But label founder J. Prince was immediately a fan. Only days after label producer Crazy C passed him the demo, J. Prince popped up at the group's place in the 3rd Ward offering a chicken lunch and a recording contract. It eventually turned out to be one of the most expensive albums released by his label, thanks to the trio's tendency to write entire songs in rented studios. The Odd Squad's odds of recouping royalties weren't aided by the multiple shots fired at radio stations that never played them. Nor did it matter. Good luck finding an FM-friendly edit to the hook of "Fa Sho'": "When you're fuckin' over yo' fo-sho pussy / Tryin' to get some mo' pussy / You'll end up with no pussy, no pussy."

The chorus was a borrowed aphorism from Devin's older brother's friend—a pragmatic seen-it-all army veteran. You laugh first, but on closer listen, "Fa Sho'" becomes one of the best anti-infidelity rap songs ever written. Just a few months after Snoop Doggy Dogg and Kurupt sneered

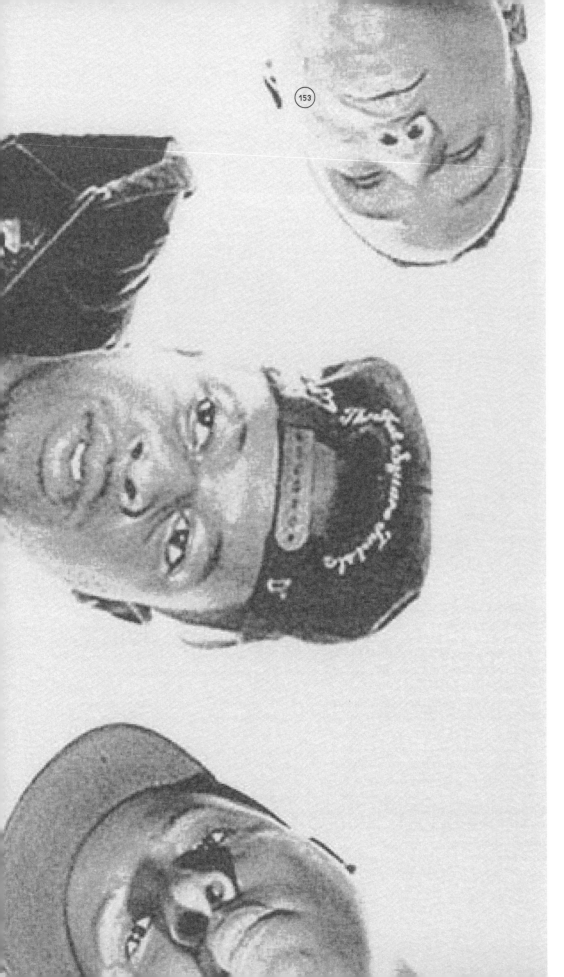

THE DEVIN
THE DUDE
COUGHEE
COMPENDIUM
*(ACCORDING
TO HIS
CATALOGUE)*

↓

PREFERRED
SMOKING
METHODS

Swisher Sweets
Zig-Zags
Black & Milds
Bongs

↓

NICKNAMES
FOR
MARIJUANA

Coughee
Cheeba
Skunk
Killa
Reefer
Doobie
Boog
Sess
Pine
K
Dank
Grass
Herb
Pot
Spinach

↓

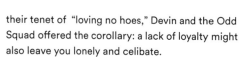

DEVIN THE DUDE PERFORMING LIVE IN PEARLAND, TEXAS, 2010

WHAT
DEVIN'S WEED
WILL GET YOU
HIGHER THAN

A rocket
A giraffe's nuts
An eagle
A choir

PHOTOGRAPH BY ZACH GARNER

RULES OF
ETIQUETTE

Don't try to hit so
hard you cough, and
you joke, and you
slob, and you fart.

Don't be babysitting
with the weed. Hit it.
Because the faster
you pass it, the faster
you get it back.

their tenet of "loving no hoes," Devin and the Odd Squad offered the corollary: a lack of loyalty might also leave you lonely and celibate.

In Squad slang, weed was "coughee," and they needed to have at least two or three cups in the morning. The code word came from a friend's dad, who clandestinely "sipped coffee" on his porch. This is part of the genius of *Fadanuf* and Devin's solo work: The subject matter rarely extends beyond smoking and sex, but the freaky tales and reincarnated wisdom make him seem part Too $hort, part Dave Chappelle, and part glazed Buddha.

With two decades of hindsight, Quest seems like the group's secret weapon. But at the time, J. Prince saw him as the centerpiece. The lone video was for "I Can't See It," a "Blind Rob" solo track

that battled his disease with raps about self-independence, beatboxing, and knocking peons out of the box. If released in New York, it would probably have been a "Stretch and Bobbito" and "Yo! MTV Raps" fixture; in Houston, it was a regionally asymmetric curio.

"It's definitely going to be something different if it's on Rap-A-Lot," says a disembodied promo voice on the album's intro track. This singularity is why *Fadanuf* holds up so well, but it's also why it was impossible to market. It captures Houston rap in chrysalis—pre-codeine and Screw—amidst its shedding of East Coast influences for an indigenous Lone Star swang.

With a few assists from Rap-A-Lot studio alchemists Mike Dean and N.O. Joe, Quest's beats merge boom-bap drums, jazz, soul samples,

"We'd smoke on some Indian tribal shit and start humming old slave spirituals," Quest says, describing the genesis of the melodies. "We'd do chants for 10 minutes straight ... almost like a trance."

viscous Southern funk, and a live saxophone lick or two. On "Hoes Wit Babies," he freaks the same Isaac Hayes sample that Public Enemy used on "Black Steel in the Hour of Chaos," while "Jazz Rendition" bows at the altars of Cannonball Adderley and The Jazz Crusaders. Quest shouts out to Showbiz and A.G. with beats hard enough to ostensibly qualify for membership in D.I.T.C., while Jugg Mugg added a necessary roughness. Devin was the star who always abides.

Unless you were a collector willing to bid triple digits on eBay, *Fadanuf Fa Erybody* was barely heard outside of Houston until the dawn of torrents. The group's only real promotion was a Midwestern Rap-A-Lot swing and three dates in Florida opening for Scarface. Even today, it's a gem often overlooked in favor of Devin's "Doobie Ashtray" era.

There was no sophomore album. Shortly after the Odd Squad began recording it, Scarface scooped up Devin for his fledgling Facemob. The Dude's solo career sparked with 1998's blunt-simple *The Dude*, but if you go through his catalog,

nearly every one of his albums features at least one Odd Squad reunion. Both of his original partners remain integral members in Devin's Coughee Brothaz clique.

"I didn't know it back then, but I know it now: I was in a group with two geniuses," says Jugg Mugg. "Rob was the brains. Devin was the heart that pumps the blood. And I was the body. We were friends first; the music was second. That's why we're still a group 20 years later, no matter what."

Maybe that quote seems a little booster-ish. But I promise that when you account for two decades of bad rap-industry contracts and backbiting, it's a miracle that any trio still records and tours together. The few who last are those with innate chemistry, who weren't formed just to get ahead. *Fadanuf Fa Erybody* is the sound of friends making the party come to them: cracking hilarious jokes, reminiscing on the previous night's debauchery, and sipping pots of coughee. The door is always wide open, and no one's ever turned away. ✍

Second-
hands

Forever 21: Animal Collective's *Sung Tongs*

With Animal Collective's warped, whooping Sung Tongs turning 10 this summer, Mike Powell looks back on his early experiences with the album as a 21-year-old college kid coming to grips with the bittersweet realities of adulthood.

Mike Powell

I first heard Animal Collective's *Sung Tongs* on an IBM ThinkPad. I'd liked their first two albums and loved their third, a chaotic live-in-the-studio set called *Here Comes the Indian*. What grabbed me about the band was the way their music blurred the line between familiar and alien forms. An Animal Collective album could sound like noise struggling to become a song, or a nursery rhyme that had been melted down and smeared across the stereo field. Listening to them was like looking at a mask: I might recognize it as a face, but I'd never mistake it for one.

This was 2004. I was 21, finishing a heady interdisciplinary program at a liberal arts school in central Virginia, tearing down long-held ideas I thought I'd understood, drinking stolen cough syrup in front of Bagel Paradise, battling it out on the hazy frontiers of the mind.[1] College is a good place to go if you don't feel like dealing with the banal realities of adulthood, which I didn't. A self-fashioned new native, I lived to conquer the world within. Everything else seemed like a dream happening somewhere outside my room, which coincidentally was a closet under a set of stairs in a house across the street from a 7-Eleven.

Animal Collective's music didn't just accompany my life, it embodied and sometimes even validated it. Here was a band that not only seemed to think that the bare fact of existence was as fucked up and confusing as I did, but also managed to replicate that confusion in sound. Biking across campus, I listened to *Sung Tongs*' alternate-reality smashes at pitiless volumes, staring at my peers, thinking, "God, it's weird to have eyeballs—could I love an insect if insects had eyeballs, too?" Naturally, my academic advisors thought I was on the right track.[2]

Sung Tongs is Animal Collective's children's album. (Here I accept that people who hate the band think all their albums are children's albums.) The songs on it are sing-alongs, rounds, lullabies—music that uses innocence to mask the ways it gets lodged in the dark parts of our brains.

It's no surprise that Animal Collective is into horror movies, which often reprise childhood fears—the bad clown, the stranger in the house—in adult contexts. The record is mostly built with acoustic guitars, live percussion, and voice, sometimes bent so far out of shape you might not be able to recognize it as human. Still, the message is clear: This is a fleshy album. An intimate album. An album that taps into myths about the things people are capable of when bonded together in a meditative state somewhere off the grid.[3][4]

At first, it embarrassed me. Men who had been covered in *The New York Times* had no business squealing like infants. But in the squealing there was the promise of a safe space, a circle of protection in which I was invited to experience feelings that didn't have a place anywhere else.

There's a reason Animal Collective's music has been compared to primal scream therapy: Both suggest that there's no such thing as progress without a little bit of carefully mediated regress.

And like anything that aimed deep, *Sung Tongs* eventually touched on sex, which, at 21, I was having as often as possible. The involuntary yips, the squishy, burbling sounds, and the way the music shuddered and twitched—it all reminded me of bodies colliding. I thought of sex as clumsy—something to fumble through, not master. A song like "Visiting Friends," the 12-minute block of slowly rippling ambience in the middle of *Sung Tongs*, always sounded more erotic to me than "Let's Get It On," because "Let's Get It On" never made room for me to feel lost. Like psychedelics, I was interested in sex not as a way of asserting myself, but as a way of letting myself dissolve.[5]

The truth is that I was scared: of graduating, of growing up, of the thought that the free play of *Sung Tongs* was behind me for good. It's a common fear, but that didn't mean I didn't feel it. So I took refuge in a band that had traveled the world but still had the guts to acknowledge how scary and exciting it felt to get on an airplane ("Kids on Holiday") or make out in public ("Good Lovin Outside"), who seemed periodically goofy but also offered the promise of restoring me to a kinder and more sensitized version of myself.

A lot of music I love streamlines complicated experiences into simple forms. Humor is a byproduct of this. Wisdom, too. Both put the complexities of life in the rearview, where I can see them a little more clearly, then refocus my eyes on the road ahead. One of the reasons *Sung Tongs* still feels so potent for me is that it isn't nostalgic for the past, but an acknowledgement that feelings we think we've moved beyond still lurk inside us, raw and in need of attention we never bother to give them. It isn't a reflection on the trauma and beauty of childhood, it's a recreation of it.[6] The love I felt for it took shape like a last gasp: The moment just before the roller coaster car creaks to the top of the track and some instinct for self-preservation strikes you numb.

Some albums seem terminal to me, like a closed circuit. Others start conversations. The calendar says *Sung Tongs* is 10 years old, but despite Animal Collective's ubiquity and influence on indie music, nobody has really picked up where they left off. Even the band—notorious for changing their template and lineup from year to year—moved on. *Feels*, which came out in 2005, marked the moment they graduated to louder, fuller music capable of reaching a big-tent crowd.[7] Gone was the porch, the backyard, the woods. It was just as well. I had less room in my schedule for acting like a five-year-old anyway. Impedances, distractions, the hard shell of sophistication—they grow and keep growing. I stopped buying my

"God, it's weird to have eyeballs— could I love an insect if insects had eyeballs, too?"

Mike Powell *has written for* Pitchfork, Grantland, Rolling Stone, *and a variety of other print and web publications. He lives in Tucson, Arizona.*

clothes by the pound, and the acid in my freezer isn't any stronger than it was when I bought it eight months ago, but I'm no closer to making time for it.

Last year I found myself waiting in the security check line at LaGuardia Airport after flying home to visit my mom. It was a good trip, bittersweet and marked by garden-variety annoyances along with moments of deep, inextricable connection. (As she likes to say, by way of both unconditional love and vague threat: "You'll always be my son.") When I got to the TSA agent, I handed over my license. For reasons I don't understand, the state of Connecticut has allowed me to keep the same photo I've had since I was 17. The agent looked confused. I asked if anything was wrong. "No," she said. "Just that you were a young man then. Now you're a grown man."

Years of unofficial training had braced me for situations like this, when tenderness hits so unexpectedly and in a context so banal that it seems like a mistake. Without thinking, I waved my hand across my body as if unveiling some game show prize and said, "Yeah, but I still got it, don't I?"

Both of us smiled, and for a second I pictured myself dropping my bags and throwing my arms around her, crying that there were days I couldn't believe I'd even made it this far. Instead, I told her to take care and have a great day, then I walked briskly toward my gate with a tight smile and my bags at my side, the way grown men do. ✐

---

[1] I've been told the bagel place was called Chesapeake Bagel and not Bagel Paradise, which I guess started as an embellishment and hardened into fact over time. Strange how that happens even when you're aware of the possibility. In any case, it's closed, though the CVS where we would steal cough syrup is still around. I always played the decoy, and bristled with excitement every time I walked through the RF detectors knowing we'd gotten away with it. After a while they started to look like goal posts.

[2] Late college was probably the first time I had a fully developed idea of how the world works and the last time I felt like I could do much about it. If I sound derisive about all this now it's only because I can't believe how certain I was then.

[3] Though generally a quartet, *Sung Tongs* only featured two of the band's members,

Avey Tare and Panda Bear. It was recorded in the cement living room of a two-bedroom house that Tare's parents owned in Lamar, Colorado, a home-rule municipality about a half hour from the Kansas border. "Home" is an important theme in Animal Collective's music. Where we make it, how we maintain it, what drives us away from it, and what pulls us inexorably back. The drum track on "Kids on Holiday" was apparently the sound of Avey Tare slamming the house's door.

[4] Necessary context here is that in the early aughts the music press had concocted a class they called "freak folk," which basically referred to young musicians who seemed to be brushing against the grain of sleekness and urbanity by going back to some perceived idea of "roots." Most of this meant pre-war folk and acoustic psychedelia from the late '60s. Unplugged instruments, simple living, the

way one's humanity returns to them when sitting cross-legged on a log in the middle of the woods—this was the myth. "We didn't party so much," Avey Tare told *Arthur* magazine in 2005, in a conversation about his childhood. "We lived in a forested area. Driving around the Maryland countryside listening to The Incredible String Band, that's what I connected music to."

[5] Animal Collective was always reticent to talk about drugs, paying deference to their power while being careful to make clear that their music didn't depend on them. "It's work," Geologist told *Free Williamsburg* in 2005, burned out on the question years before most people were even paying attention to them.

[6] I recently dug up an email exchange between me and an old girlfriend—or, more accurately, my first love, a person built so deeply into who I am that I don't think I'll ever be

able to successfully remove her without the whole house falling down. At the time, we were living in different states—her in North Carolina, me in New York. It was February 2005, and she'd just seen Animal Collective for the first time. Her report in full: "I feel more."

[7] I remember seeing them on a narrow stage in the basement of a sushi restaurant in Virginia in 2004, a few months before *Sung Tongs* came out. When I say basement, I mean basement— low ceilings, exposed pipes, cement floors. Less than a year later I saw them in New York at Webster Hall, a Queen Anne ballroom with a capacity of about 1,400, and remember thinking how tiny and inconsequential they looked on such a grand stage. By the time they played "Banshee Beat"—from *Feels*, which hadn't yet come out—I realized they were going to get much bigger than they were.